Dear Reader

I have always been fascinated by the lives of pioneers—the men who were brave enough, strong enough, determined enough to take on a harsh, dangerous and alien land and forge a future for themselves and their families. To me such men are a very special breed.

Two years ago I wrote a trilogy about the **Kings of the Outback** from the Kimberly, a family who had become legendary in that vast expanse of Australia. Another part of Australia which tested the grit and endurance of pioneers is the tropical far north of Queensland. Instead of drought, they faced cyclones; instead of desert, almost impenetrable rainforest. Yet the land was cleared for profitable plantations—sugar cane, tea, tropical fruit.

I decided to marry one of the King men from the Kimberly to a remarkable Italian woman, Isabella Valeri, whose father had pioneered the far north. This trilogy is about their three grandsons—Alex, Tony and Matt—and the women they choose to partner them into their future.

These men are a very special breed. Nothing will stop them from winning what they want. I love reading about men like that. I hope you do, too.

With love

Emma Da

Award-winning Australian author **Emma Darcy** writes compelling, sexy, intensely emotional novels that have gripped the imagination of readers around the globe. She's written an impressive 80 novels for Modern Romance® and sold nearly 60 million books worldwide.

Welcome to the thrilling climax of Emma Darcy's exciting new trilogy:

KINGS OF AUSTRALIA

**The King brothers must marry—
can they claim the brides of their choice?**

Alessandro, Antonio and Matteo
are three gorgeous brothers and heirs
to a plantation empire in the lush tropical
north of Australia. Each must find a bride
to continue the prestigious family line…
but will they marry for duty, passion, or love?

June 2002: **THE ARRANGED MARRIAGE**
July 2002: **THE BRIDAL BARGAIN**
August 2002: **THE HONEYMOON CONTRACT**

If you'd like to share your thoughts on
the **KINGS OF AUSTRALIA** do write to:
The Editor, Harlequin Mills & Boon Ltd., Eton House,
18-24 Paradise Road, Richmond, Surrey TW9 1SR

THE HONEYMOON CONTRACT

BY
EMMA DARCY

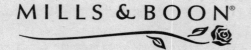

MILLS & BOON®

First published in Great Britain 2002
Harlequin Mills & Boon Limited,
Eton House, 18-24 Paradise Road, Richmond, Surrey TW9 1SR

© Emma Darcy 2002

ISBN 0 263 82952 9

Set in Times Roman 10½ on 12½ pt.
01-0802-41168

Printed and bound in Spain
by Litografia Rosés, S.A., Barcelona

CHAPTER ONE

MATT KING had spent a highly satisfying day, white-water rafting on the Tully River with his friends. It was good to be single and unattached, free to enjoy fun and games anytime he liked. At thirty, Matt figured he had a few more carefree bachelor years up his sleeve before marriage became a serious item on his agenda and he was not about to fall victim to any plans his grandmother might have to get him wed.

Today's activity had been the perfect excuse not to turn up at the Sunday luncheon she had organized for the purpose of introducing her latest female protégée to the family. Matt knew it was only delaying the inevitable. Sooner or later he would have to meet this Nicole Redman. He could hardly avoid her for the whole six months she was under contract to write the family history, especially as she was staying as *a guest* at King's Castle for the duration. Nevertheless, he was determined not to dance to his grandmother's tune.

The telephone rang just as he was about to settle down and watch a bit of television before going to bed. Feeling at peace with his world, and pleased with the neat little sidestep he'd performed today, Matt even smiled indulgently when he heard his grandmother's voice on the other end of the line.

"Ah! You are safely home, Matteo," she said, letting him know she disapproved of dangerous pursuits that risked life and limb for no good reason.

"Yes, Nonna. I managed not to drown or break any bones," he answered cheerfully.

"More good luck than good management," she muttered darkly before moving to the real point of her call. "Will you be in your bus depot office in the morning?"

No ducking out of this one, Matt thought. Business was business and his grandmother knew his work routine. Midweek he moved around the tropical fruit plantations but Mondays and Fridays were spent with the transport company he'd developed himself, picking up the tourist dollar in a big way.

"Yes," he replied to the lead-in question, waiting for the crunch.

"Good! I'll send Nicole along to you. I want you to give her a gold pass so she can travel freely on any of your bus tours."

"Doesn't she have a car?" Matt asked very dryly, knowing he was about to be outmanoeuvred but putting in a token protest anyway.

"Yes. But the bus tours will give her a general feel of the area she will have to cover in her research and your drivers do give potted histories as they go."

"More gossip than fact, Nonna. The aim is to entertain, not cram with information."

"It adds a certain flavour that is distinctive to far North Queensland, Matteo. Since Nicole is not familiar with Port Douglas or its environs, I don't see it as a waste of time.''

''A pity you didn't employ someone local who wouldn't have to start from scratch,'' he remarked.

''Nicole Redman had the qualifications I wanted for this project,'' came the definitive reply.

''Nothing beats local knowledge,'' he argued, strongly suspecting *the qualifications* had very little to do with writing a family history.

He was awake to his grandmother's matchmaking game. His two older brothers hadn't twigged to it and here they were, neatly married off to brides of their choice, or so they thought. Not that Matt had any quarrel with the women they'd wed. Gina and Hannah were beautiful people. It was just that he now knew they'd been Nonna's choices for Alex and Tony before his brothers had even met them.

Good thing he'd overheard her triumphant conversation with Elizabeth King at Tony's wedding, plus the voiced hope that she would be able to find a suitable wife for her third grandson. Matt had little doubt that Nicole Redman was the selected candidate.

She probably didn't know it, any more than he was supposed to know it, but that didn't change the game. Her arrival on the family scene repeated the previous pattern of his grandmother employing a young woman who ended up married to one of her grandsons. Since *he* was the only one left unmarried...

''Many people can do research and write down a list of facts, Matteo,'' his grandmother declared in a tone of arch disdain, applying her authority in no uncertain terms. "Having the skill to tell a story well is something else. I do not want an amateurish publication. This is important to me."

It was pure Isabella Valeri King…not to be denied. Even at eighty years of age she was still a formidable character and Matt loved and respected her far too much not to give in…a little.

"Sorry, Nonna. Of course it is," he quickly conceded. "You know best what you want and if a gold bus pass will help the project, I'm only too happy to assist."

It would only take a minute of his time. A brief meeting during business hours—no social obligation attached to it—would serve to satisfy his curiosity about what made Nicole Redman *suitable* for him in his grandmother's eyes.

"I thought you could also supply the road maps she will need when she does venture out by herself. Explain the various areas of particular family interest to her and how best to get there."

Matt could see the minute stretching to half an hour but there was no way he could refuse this reasonable request. "Okay. I'll have them ready for her." With all the plantations marked on them from Cape Tribulation to Innisfail. That would save time and evade the cosy togetherness his grandmother was undoubtedly plotting.

"Thank you, Matteo. When would be most convenient for Nicole to call by?"

Never. He suppressed the telling word and answered, "Oh, let's say ten-thirty."

The call ended on that agreement and for quite some time afterwards, Matt mused on how very clever his grandmother was, keeping strictly to business, no hint of trying to push any personal interest, not even a comment on Nicole Redman as a person, simply pressing a meeting which was reasonably justified.

Could he be wrong about this plot?

No, it still fitted the modus operandi.

His grandmother had produced Gina Terlizzi, a wedding singer, just as Alex was planning his wedding to a woman his grandmother didn't like. With good reason, Matt had to concede. He hadn't liked Michelle Banks, either, and was glad Alex had married Gina instead. Nevertheless, it was definitely his grandmother's guiding hand behind the meetings which had brought the desired result.

Then she had trapped Tony very neatly, choosing Hannah O'Neill to be the new chef on his prized catamaran, *Duchess*. Never mind about her highly questionable qualifications to be a cook. Tony had made the mistake of giving their grandmother the task of interviewing the applicants and making the choice, which had allowed her to present him with a *fait accompli* which sealed his fate. Impossible to ignore Hannah's other qualifications when they were inescapably right in his face. Tony had been down for the count in no time flat.

Two protégées married to his brothers.

Third one coming up.

Nicole Redman had to be aimed at him. The only question was…what ammunition did she have to shoot him into the marriage stakes? It certainly added a piquant interest to tomorrow morning's meeting.

He grinned with easy confidence as he switched on the television.

Didn't matter what it was, he was proofed against it. There was not going to be a honeymoon contract attached to the contract Nicole Redman had with his grandmother. No way was *he* ready to get married!

12   THE HONEYMOON CONTRACT

CHAPTER TWO

NICOLE paused at the head of the steps that led down to Wharf Street and looked back at King's Castle, marvelling that such a place had been built here back in the pioneering days. Tropical North Queensland was a long way from Rome, yet Frederico Stefano Valeri, Isabella's father, had certainly stuck to his Italian heritage when constructing this amazing villa on top of the hill overlooking Port Douglas.

The locals had come to call it a castle because of the tesselated tower that provided the perfect lookout in every direction, but the loggia and the fountain had definitely been inspired by Roman villas. And all of it built with poured concrete, a massive feat in those early times, although no doubt Frederico, having seen the timber buildings of Port Douglas destroyed in the 1911 cyclone, had been intent on having his home stand against anything.

Home and family, Nicole thought, her mind turning to the two great-grandsons she had met yesterday, both of them exuding the kind of strength that would tackle any problem and come out on top. The sense of family heritage and tradition was very much alive in them, nurtured no doubt by their extraordinary grandmother. It would be interesting to see if their younger brother fitted the same mould.

Three brothers—Alessandro, Antonio, Matteo—carrying the past into the future, adding to the levels of enterprise that had been started by Frederico when he had left Italy to start a new life in Australia in 1906. A fascinating family with a fascinating history and an equally fascinating present, Nicole decided, turning away from the castle to continue her walk to the KingTours head office.

It was only ten o'clock in the morning but already the heat was beating through her wide-brimmed straw hat. All too easy to get sunstroke up here in the tropics, she'd been warned, so she kept to the shade of the trees bordering the road on her leisurely stroll down the hill to the main business centre. Given her very fair skin, she had to protect herself against sunburn, as well. It was to be hoped the block-out cream she'd lavished on her arms and legs would do the job.

Being a redhead did have drawbacks in a country devoted to sunshine and outdoor pursuits. It was lucky she had always loved books, reading and writing being her dearest pleasures. Staying indoors had never really been a hardship, plus living with her father for the last few years of his life had left her with the habit of being a night owl—a habit she had to change while working with Isabella Valeri King.

Still, that was no real hardship, either. There was a special brilliancy to the days in Port Douglas; the magic of sunrise over the ocean, the kind of sharp daylight that made colours more vibrant. One never saw green this *green* in Sydney, and the reds and oranges and yellows of the tropical flowers were quite wonderful.

Everything was different; the whole laid-back pace of the town, no sense of hustle and bustle, the heat of the day followed by a downpour of incredibly heavy rain most afternoons. It spurred an awareness of nature and the need to live in harmony with it. She felt a long long way from city life, as though she'd moved to another world that worked within parameters all its own. It was a very attractive world that could easily become addictive.

Here she was, swinging along at a very leisurely pace, flat sandals on her feet, no stockings, wearing a yellow sleeveless button-through dress that loosely skimmed her body, minimal underclothing, a straw hat featuring a big yellow sunflower on her head, and it didn't matter what anyone thought of her. No students to teach, no fellow academics pushing their political agendas at her, no back-biting about the book she'd written on her father's life.

Freedom…

She grinned, happy with the feeling. It was like starting a new life even though she'd be researching old lives for the next six months, writing a history. But it was a history *she* hadn't lived and it was about a family who had endured and survived and was still thriving, the kind of family she didn't have and had never known. Another attraction…finding out first-hand what it was like to actually belong to a place, deep roots and long lines of growth.

She reached Macrossan Street and strolled along it until she found the King building where Alessandro—Alex, as he was called by everyone except his grandmother and Rosita, the very motherly Italian housekeeper at the castle—managed investments and property development, as well as handling all the business attached to the sugarcane plantations.

Further down Wharf Street was the marina where Antonio/Tony operated the Kingtripper line of catamarans, taking tourists out to the Great Barrier Reef. That was his personal enterprise, apart from managing the tea plantations which was his family responsibility. Nicole intended to check out the Kingtripper company office after her meeting with Matteo/Matt.

She turned into Owen Street which led down to the bus depot and the KingTours main office. The transport company was Matt's brainchild and one of the tours he ran was to his exotic fruit farm, an extension of the tropical fruit plantations that came under his umbrella of family responsibility.

It was interesting that none of the three brothers had simply accepted their inheritances and been content to live off them. Which they could have done, given the current prosperity of all the plantations. Of course, diversity was always a healthier situation in any financial sense, but Nicole suspected the pioneering blood ran strongly in these men. Perhaps it was the challenge of going for more that drove them. Or a *male* thing, wanting to conquer new territories.

Certainly Alex and Tony King were different to all the city men she'd known. They were very civilised, very polished in their manners, yet they had a masculinity that was somehow more aggressive. In her mind's eye she could see the two of them going into battle, shoulder to shoulder, emanating the attitude that nothing was going to beat them. Perhaps it was fanciful imagination but that was how they had impressed her.

Would the third brother measure up to the other two?

It was with a very lively anticipation that Nicole stepped into the KingTours main office. A fresh-faced boy, possibly in his late teens, was manning a large L-shaped desk. He looked up from his paperwork, gave her a quick once-over, then a welcoming grin.

"You Miss Redman?"

"Yes."

He waved to a door in the back wall to the side of his desk. "Just step this way to the boss's office. He's got all the maps ready for you." His blue eyes twinkled as though that statement reflected some private joke. "I marked out the main locations of interest myself so you can't possibly miss them," he added, making Nicole wonder if he'd been told to assume she was the most hopeless navigator in the world.

He already had the door open for her so there was no time to chat with him. "Miss Redman," he was announcing, even before she thought to remove her hat.

Indeed, the ushering was effected so quickly, Nicole

found herself inside Matt King's office with her hat still on and her wits completely scattered at being confronted by the man himself. Not like Alex. Not like Tony. This brother was wickedly handsome. If the devil was rolling out every sexual temptation he could load into a male body, Matt King had to be his masterpiece.

His hair was very black, very shiny and an absolute riot of tight curls, a tantalising invitation to be touched. It didn't soften the strong masculine cast of his face. Somehow the contrast added a wildly mischievous attraction, as did the long, thick, curly eyelashes to the dark chocolate eyes. And his olive skin had such a smooth sheen, the pads of Nicole's fingers actually prickled with the desire to stroke it. All that on top of a physique that seemed to pulse manpower at her.

He came out from behind his desk, tall, big, dressed in a blue sports shirt and navy chinos, white teeth flashing at her, and Nicole felt as though every bit of oxygen had been punched out of her lungs. Her heart catapulted around a chest that had suddenly become hollow. It was purely a defensive instinct that lifted her hands to grab her hat and bring it down in front of her like a shield against the impact of his approach.

The action startled him into pausing and Nicole's cheeks flamed with embarrassment. Such a clumsy thing to do, no grace at all in this foolish fluster. And she'd probably mussed her hair. He was staring at it. A slight frown drew his brows together as his gaze dropped to hers, his eyes brilliantly sharp now, seemingly as black as his hair and with a penetrating power that felt so invasive it made her toes curl.

She had the weird sense he was searching for some sign of recognition. It forced her to collect her wits and speak, though her tongue moved sluggishly and she had to push the words out. "Your grandmother sent me. I'm Nicole Redman."

"Red..." he said with an ironic twist, then appeared to recover himself. "Forgive me for staring. That shade of hair is not exactly common. It surprised me." He stepped forward and offered his hand. "Matt King."

She unlatched the fingers of her right hand from the hat and gingerly met his grasp. "I'm pleased to meet you," she managed stiltedly, absorbing the shock wave of his engulfing touch with as much control as she could muster. A bolt of warm, tingling vitality shot up her arm and caused her heart to pump harder.

His gaze dropped to her mouth, studying it as though it held secrets she was not revealing. Her throat constricted, making further speech impossible.

"Nicole Redman..." He rolled her name out slowly, as though tasting it for flavour and texture. His gaze flicked back to hers, his eyes having gathered a mocking gleam. "This meeting is overdue but no doubt we'll soon get acquainted."

He had to be referring to his absence from the family luncheon yesterday, yet that look in his eyes was implying more. Mental confusion added to her physical tension and it was a blessed relief when he withdrew his hand and turned aside to fetch a chair for her, placing it to face his on the other side of the executive desk.

''Have a seat,'' he invited, and Nicole was intensely grateful for it.

Her knees felt like jelly. Her thighs were quivering, too. She found the presence of mind to say, ''Thank you,'' and sank onto the chair, fiercely telling herself to construct some composure fast.

It wasn't as though she hadn't been given a hint of what Matt King might be like, having met his brothers yesterday, both very handsome men who carried an aura of power. She had been able to view them objectively. Why not this one? Why did she feel so personally affected by this one?

It was crazy. She was twenty-eight years old and had met hundreds of men. Probably thousands. Not one of them had scrambled her insides like this. Maybe she was suffering sunstroke and just didn't know it. Come to think of it, she did feel slightly dizzy. And very hot. Hot all over. If she just sat quietly for a minute or two, she'd be fine.

She slid her shoulder-bag off and propped it against the leg of the chair, then set her hat on her lap and focused on the sunflower. By the time Matt King reached his chair and settled himself to chat with her, she'd be ready to look at him and act normally.

All she needed from him was the gold pass for the bus tours and the road maps which his assistant had helpfully marked. It shouldn't take hardly any time at all. A bit of polite to-and-fro and she'd be out of here.

Her hands were trembling.

She willed them to be still.

Her heart persisted with hops, skips and jumps, but it had to steady soon. Clearly she had to be more careful in this tropical heat. Drive, not walk. That was the answer. When Matt King spoke to her she would look up and smile and everything would be all right.

CHAPTER THREE

No MISTAKE, Matt grimly assured himself as he walked slowly around his desk to his chair, his mind working at hyper-speed to reason out what the hell this woman was doing here, supposedly assisting his grandmother on the family history project.

The flaming red hair had instantly jolted his memory, spinning it back ten years to a night in New Orleans, the night before Halloween in that extraordinary city. The delicately featured face, the white porcelain-perfect skin, the big expressive sherry-brown eyes, the full sensual curves of her mobile mouth...all of it like a video clip coming at him in a flash. A tall slender young woman, swathed in a black cloak lined with purple satin, long red hair flowing free, not rolled back at the sides and clipped away from her face as it was today.

He'd seen her lecturing the tour group outside Reverend Zombie's Voodoo Shop. He'd watched her, listened to her, appreciating the theatrical appearance of her as she captivated the group with her opening spiel for the Haunted History Walking Tour. Just to hear her speaking in an Australian accent added to her allure.

He'd even tagged along for a while, fascinated by the look of her and her performance. He would probably have stayed with it but the novelty appeal of the tour soon wore thin for the friends he was with and they'd moved on to one of the colourful bars in the French Quarter.

Nevertheless, he remembered her very clearly...the hair, the face, the pale, pale skin adding its impact to her ghostly tales. Which raised the question...what tale had she spun his grandmother to get this job? Had she faked qualifications...a con-woman getting her hooks in for a six months' free ride? Had his grandmother checked them out? Or hadn't they mattered, given that her prime objective was finding him a bride?

A spurt of anger put an extra edge on the tension this meeting had sparked. His grandmother had struck out badly on this candidate for marital bliss, being fooled by what he could only think of as a fly-by-night operator, though undoubtedly a very clever and convincing one, calling on her experience with *haunted history,* plus a liberal dash of entertainment.

He slung himself into his chair, barely resisting the urge to give it a twirl as a derisive tribute to the marriage merry-go-round his grandmother was intent upon. Highly disgruntled with this absurd situation, he glowered at the woman sitting opposite to him. *Why her?* What did his grandmother see as the special attributes that made *her* suitable as his wife?

Red hair?

It certainly suited the exotic night-life in New Orleans, but here in the tropics? That pale skin would fry in Port Douglas. Utter madness!

Though he had to concede her dramatic colouring and

the delicacy of her fine skin and features did have a certain unique beauty. He'd thought so ten years ago and it still held true. But it was perfectly plain she didn't belong in this environment. As to there being any possibility of her spending a lifetime here...that was definitely beyond the pale.

She sat very still, very primly with her knees pressed together, the hat held on her lap, eyes downcast, projecting a modesty that was at ridiculous odds with the role she had played ten years ago. Uncloaked, she had small but neatly rounded breasts. Her arms were neatly rounded, too, slender like the rest of her but not skinny. Interesting that she wore yellow, which wasn't a modest colour.

She was playing some game with him, Matt decided, and the temptation to winkle it out of her overrode his previous intention to send her on her way as quickly as possible. He leaned back in his chair and consciously relaxed, knowing he had the upper hand since there was no chance of her remembering him. He and his friends had been wearing masks that night, part of the wild revelry leading up to Halloween.

"I understand this is your first visit to the far north," he started.

She nodded and slowly raised her gaze to his. "I did fly up a month ago for the interview with Mrs. King."

Her eyes were wary and he instantly sensed her guard was up against him. He wondered why. A need to hide the truth about herself? Did she see him as a danger spot, a threat to her cosy sinecure at the castle?

Curiosity further piqued, he smiled to put her more at ease as he teasingly asked, ''Six months at the castle didn't sound like a prison sentence to you?''

The idea seemed to startle her. ''Not at all. Why would you think so?''

''Oh, you'll be stuck mostly with my grandmother for company and the novelty of living in a rather romantic old place won't make up for the things you'll miss or the things you'll have to tolerate,'' he drawled, watching her reaction to his words.

Her head tilted to one side as though she was critically assessing him. ''Don't *you* enjoy your grandmother's company?''

''That's not exactly relevant,'' he dryly countered.

A slight frown. ''You didn't come to the family luncheon yesterday.''

''True. I don't allow my grandmother to rule my life. I had another activity booked and I saw no reason to cancel it.'' He paused, wanting to probe her character. ''Were you offended that I didn't roll up on command?''

''Me? Of course not.''

''Then why do you think I should have come?''

''I don't. I just thought…you said…'' She stopped in some confusion.

''I was simply suggesting that six months under the same roof with an eighty-year-old lady might make King's Castle a prison for a young woman used to all the attractions of city life.''

A wry little smile. ''Actually I find older people more interesting than younger ones. They've lived longer and some of them have had amazing lives. I can't imagine ever being bored in Mrs. King's company.''

Her eyes flashed a look that suggested she could very easily be bored in his, which spurred him into derisively commenting, ''So you're prepared to bury yourself in the past and let your own life slide by for the duration of this project.''

Her chin tilted in challenge. ''I've always found history fascinating. I think there's much to be learnt from it. I don't consider any form of learning a waste of my time.''

''A very academic view,'' he pointed out, wondering what she'd *learnt* from ghost stories. ''They say history repeats itself, so what really is gleaned from it?'' he challenged right back. ''Human nature doesn't change.''

She didn't reply. For several moments she looked directly at him in a silence loaded with antagonism. She wanted to attack. So did he. But his grandmother stood between them, a force that demanded a stay of any open hostilities.

''Are you against this project, Matt?''

The question was put quietly, calmly, a straight request to know where he stood.

''Not in the slightest. I think such a publication will be of interest to future generations of our family,'' he answered easily. ''I think it's also meaningful to my grandmother to have a record of her life put into print. A last testament, which she richly deserves.''

''Are you against me doing it?''

Right on target! He had to hand it to Nicole Redman.

She certainly had balls to lay the cards right out on the table. "Why should I be?" he asked, wondering if she'd let anything slip.

"I don't know." Another wry little smile. "You'll need to tell me."

Clever, throwing the question back onto him. "How old are you Nicole?" he tossed at her.

"Twenty-eight."

"Are you coming out of a bad relationship?"

"No."

"Not engaged with one at the moment?"

"No."

"Not looking for one?"

"No."

"Why not?"

"Why should I be?"

"I would have thought it was a normal pastime for a woman of your age."

Hot colour stained her cheeks. Her eyes burned with pride as she replied, "Then I guess I don't fit your idea of normal."

Which neatly left him nothing to say...on the surface of it. He was not about to fire his hidden ammunition until he knew some facts about her more recent circumstances. A lot could happen in ten years. If she was telling the truth about her age, she'd only been eighteen in New Orleans. A wild youth could have been followed by a more sober settling down.

As it was, she had obviously notched up qualifications in his grandmother's wedding plans; single, unattached, of a mature enough age to find marriage an acceptable idea, and certainly physically attractive if one fancied red hair.

Not everybody did.

So why had his grandmother chosen a redhead for him? Why not a blonde or brunette? He'd never even…

The answer suddenly clicked in. Trish at Tony's wedding. Hannah's sister had long auburn hair and he'd been matched with her in the wedding party, bridesmaid and groomsman. Being a professional model, she was tall and slender, too, and they'd had a lot of fun together at the reception. No serious connection, just light happy flirting, enjoyed by both of them. Had his grandmother read more into it, perceiving Trish as his type of woman?

He shook his head and Nicole took the exasperated action as directed at her.

"This is a project I want to do," she stated, her eyes mocking his assertion that looking for a man should be her top priority. "I understand from Mrs. King that you started this tour company because you wanted to do it. You've also developed a market for exotic fruit, which I assume you wanted to do, as well. I'm sure you had your reasons for taking those directions in your life and I bet they had nothing to do with your lack of, or desire for, a relationship with a woman."

She had him there. This was one smart chick. If he so much as suggested it might be different for a woman, he'd be marked as a sexist pig. Besides, he didn't believe it was different. He'd simply been checking what his grandmother had undoubtedly checked before entering Nicole Redman in her matchmaking game.

"Well, I hope you find as much satisfaction in pursuing the past as I've found in setting up a future," he said with a grin designed to disarm.

She returned an overly sweet smile. "You're very fortunate to have a past that can be built upon."

The slip! It was in her eyes, a bleak emptiness that had escaped her guard. His instincts instantly seized upon it and threw up a quick interpretation. She'd come from nothing and had no future direction. She moved on the wings of opportunity, not having any roots to ground her anywhere. Perhaps she even felt like a ghost, having no family to give her any real solidity. Or was he assuming too much from one fleeting expression?

"What about your own family?" he shot out.

"I don't have one," she answered flatly, confirming his impression.

"You're an orphan?"

A momentary gritting of teeth, then a terse dismissal of that description of her. "I'm an adult, responsible for myself, and I've taken the responsibility of seeing this project through with Mrs. King. A six-month contract has been signed to that effect. If you have a problem with my appointment to this job…"

"It's purely my grandmother's business and I have no intention of interfering with it," he assured her, though whether his grandmother would get value for her choice on the history side of things was yet to be seen.

Nevertheless, that was not his problem and he wasn't about to make it his problem.

"I don't want to interfere with your business, either." She surged up from her chair with the clear intention of making a brisk departure. "Your assistant said you had road maps already marked for me…"

Damn! He'd torpedoed any reason for keeping her with him. Had to go with the flow now. He killed the stab of frustration and rose to his feet, telling himself he had six months to get to the bottom of this woman, so no sweat about letting her off the hook this morning.

He picked up the bundle of maps stacked on his side of the desk and set them on her side. "Here they are," he said obligingly. "Using these, you should be able to find your way to every point of historical interest."

"Thank you." She scooped her bag from the floor and rested it on the desk to load the maps into it, her face closed to everything but the purpose that had brought her to him.

Matt didn't like the sense of being put out of Nicole Redman's picture. He wasn't ready to let her go…*to let her win*. He snatched up the gold bus pass he'd laid beside the maps and strolled around the desk, intent on forcing another passage of play.

"And this gives you free travel on any of the tours," he said, holding it out to her.

She jerked towards him, a couple of the maps spilling out of her hand. In her quick fumble to catch them, she dropped her hat. They both bent to pick it up, their heads almost bumping. She reared back, leaving Matt to retrieve it, which he did, straightening up to find her breathing fast and very flustered by the near collision.

Her mouth was slightly open, her eyes wide in alarm, and this close to her, Matt had the weird sensation of being sucked in by the storm of feeling coming straight at him from the highly luminous windows to her soul. He stared back, momentarily transfixed by a connection that threw him completely out of kilter.

He wanted to kiss her, wanted to draw from her mouth all the secrets she was hiding from him, wanted to bind her to him until she gave up everything she was. The need to know pounded through his mind. Adrenaline was rushing through him, making his heart beat faster, tightening his muscles, driving a fierce urge for satisfaction. An intensely *sexual* urge for satisfaction.

''Thank you.''

The words whispered from her lips.

They forced a realisation of what he was supposed to be doing. Shock pummelled the madness out of his mind. This was the woman his grandmother had lined up for him. He was *not* going to fall into her trap.

He thrust out the gold pass.

Her hand was trembling as she took it from him. He tried to rein in the wild burst of energy that had escaped from him. Was she aware of it, affected by it? One part of him savagely hoped so, even as another part just as savagely wanted to deny there was any power of attraction in operation here, on her side or his.

He watched her shove the pass and the maps into the bag, lashes lowered, head bowed, the red of her hair so vibrant he had to clench his hands to stop them from reaching out to touch it. They clenched over the straw brim of her hat. He still had the hat. But it was crazy even thinking he could hold her hostage with a hat. Her haste in packing her bag, slinging it over her shoulder, said she wanted to go. And he should let her go. Any other action would put him well and truly in the loser's seat.

She managed a step away, increasing the distance between them as she turned to face him, her gaze flicking up in frazzled appeal. "My hat…"

He could have handed it to her. It was the simplest response. But some perverse aggressive streak goaded him into setting the hat on that taunting hair himself, as though covering up the temptation would make it go away. He stepped forward and did precisely that, fitting the crown of the hat on her head, focusing on the sunflower to position it as she'd had it positioned when she came in, an unknown woman he'd intended to remain unknown to him in any close personal sense.

Except his whole body was suddenly electrically aware of hers, her height against his, the slightness of her figure, the almost fragile femininity of it, the yellow of the sunflower reminding her of her dress—a button-through dress that could be easily opened—and she was standing so still, submissively still.

"Thank you."

A gush of breath. Had she been holding it?

The thought excited him. He'd won something from

her. On a heady wave of triumph he stepped back, smiling. "Got to be careful of the heat up here."

Her cheeks were reflecting an inner heat that put him on a high as he moved to open the office door for her exit. She walked forward with the stiff gait of someone willing her legs into action. Her gaze was fixed on the doorway. She gave him a nod of acknowledgment as she passed by.

Matt grinned as he closed the door behind her.

He'd definitely rattled Nicole Redman's cage.

And he certainly felt a zing of interest in opening the door to it.

Not to marry her, he assured himself as he headed back to his desk. Marriage was not on his agenda. But a few hot nights with Miss Exotic New Orleans would not go amiss. Why not...if she fancied a taste of the tropics? Not under the nose of his grandmother, of course, but if Nicole was doing all the bus tours, sooner or later she would take the trip to Kauri King Park where the exotic fruit was grown.

He would make a point of being there that day.

And see how he felt about her then.

CHAPTER FOUR

As was her habit, Isabella Valeri King took afternoon tea in the loggia by the fountain. The sound of flowing water was soothing. There was always a sea-breeze at this time of day to alleviate the heat. She liked being outside with so much of her world to view, its changing colours, changing light, the sense of being part of it, still alive, though not with as much life left to live as the young woman sitting with her.

Nicole Redman...

So different to Gina and Hannah both in looks and nature, yet she shared with them the quality Isabella most admired—the inner strength to make hard life decisions and follow them through. The book about her father had revealed much about herself—a child who had shouldered the responsibility of an adult, seeing the gain, setting aside the loss—a very mature view for one so young.

Though she had suffered loss.

Just as Isabella had.

The past two hours in the library, reliving the years of the Second World War through old photographs and letters, had left her feeling heavy-hearted. She'd lost both her husband and only brother to that dreadful conflict in Europe, and there'd been other troubles, many of the Italian immigrants in far North Queensland interned because they had not taken out Australian citizenship as her parents had.

Her father had done his best to ease that pain in the Italian community, making a deal with the government, offering land he owned as a suitable camp for *his people,* then talking the forestry department into supplying the plants and trees to construct a rainforest park there, arguing the conservation of tropical species as well as keeping the internees occupied by the work. Better than useless imprisonment. Something good would come of it for everyone.

"After the war, you and Edward can build a home up there, Isabella," he'd told her.

But Edward hadn't come back from the war and Kauri King Park, as it came to be known, had never been her home. It was now Matteo's, and Nicole had not yet been there. Which brought Isabella's focus back to the young woman who had been with her for almost three weeks now.

Only the one meeting with Matteo.

A pity she had been unable to observe it.

Perhaps there would have been nothing to observe. The beauty she saw in Nicole may not have appealed to Matteo. He had made no attempt to pursue an acquaintance with her. Nor had Nicole made any comments that would have revealed a personal interest in him.

Isabella silently conceded the undeniable truth that one could not order mutual attraction. Physical chemistry was ordained by nature and no amount of wanting it to happen could *make* it happen. However, it was curious that Nicole had soaked in the background information from many of Matteo's bus tours, yet had not so far chosen to take the one tour which might bring her into contact with him. Since it was also the one tour most closely connected to the family history, why was she putting it off?

To Isabella's mind it smacked of avoidance. Which could mean something about Matteo moved Nicole out of her comfort zone. A negative reaction? Had Matteo offended her in some way?

Her youngest grandson was not normally an abrasive person. He had a happy, fun-loving personality, very agreeable company to most people. He carried his passions lightly although they ran every bit as deeply as his two older brothers'. The lightness was his way of carving a different niche in the family.

Alessandro…the strong pillar of responsibility.

Antonio…the fierce competitor.

Matteo…the nimble dancer between the other two, pretending to skate through life as though it was a game to be played, but he did care about his responsibilities and he was every bit as competitive as Antonio. He just expressed it differently.

Maybe something had happened between Matteo and Nicole that neither of them wanted to acknowledge. An unexpected chemistry could be uncomfortable, disturbing their sense of control over their lives. Matteo liked to stir things along for other people but he was very much in charge of himself. As for Nicole…she sat with an air of tranquility which was probably hard-won, given all she'd been through. A storm of feeling might tear at nerves that craved peace.

Wishful thinking, Isabella chided herself. Whatever the situation, the history project had to stay on track and it was time for Nicole to see what they had just been talking about.

"Tomorrow I must spend on the organisation of a wedding," she stated. "The bride and her mother are coming to decide on all the details for the reception in the ballroom."

Nicole smiled. "I can't imagine a more romantic setting, having a wedding here at the castle."

"In the old days we held dances and showed movies in the ballroom. I did not want it to fall into disuse so I turned it into a function centre many years ago. Weddings are so popular here, it is used for little else now."

"I'm sure it adds very much to the sense of occasion for the couples getting married."

"I think so. The feeling of longevity is good. It makes something solid of the passage of time. As you'll see when you visit Kauri King Park. Tomorrow would be a good day for you to do that tour, Nicole, since I've just been telling you how it came to be."

The tour that would take her to Matteo's home.

There were instant signs of tension—Nicole's shoulders jerking into a straighter line, hands clenching in her lap, chin jutting slightly, and most interesting of all, a tide of heat rushing up her neck and flooding her cheeks.

It could not be the prospect of walking through a rain-forest park and an exotic fruit plantation causing such a reaction. If it was the prospect of encountering Matteo…well, perhaps more meetings should be planned.

Isabella waited for Nicole's response.

A fine hand had to be played here.

But her heart was already lifting with hope.

"Tomorrow…" Nicole struggled to hold back a protest against the proposed arrangement. None was justifiable. She had delayed the inevitable as long as she could. There simply was no acceptable excuse for getting out of going to Matt King's territory this time, but every-thing within her recoiled from being near him again. "Yes," she forced herself to say, then clutched at a du-bious lifeline. "Though the tour could be all booked up. It's late to be calling."

"If so, you could drive up and join it at the gate. It's not far. Just above Mossman. A half hour drive at most. You won't miss much of the background chat from the bus driver," came the dismissal of any possible objec-tion.

Nicole's stomach contracted. She had to do it. No es-cape. All she could hope for was Matt King's absence.

"Tomorrow is a good day," Mrs. King ran on. "Mat-teo is always there on Thursdays. He can help out with anything you'd like to know."

It was the worst possible day and she'd now been trapped into it. Her own stupid fault for not going before when she could have avoided meeting him. She knew he was in the tour company office on Mondays and Fridays. The problem was, she hadn't felt safe about going on any day.

If Matt King checked the tour bookings—and she'd had an uneasy feeling he would check on what she was up to—he could waylay her on his home ground whenever she went. Why, she wasn't sure, but everything about him put her on edge. And he knew it, played on it, getting under her skin. She didn't like it, didn't want it.

"I wouldn't want to take him away from his work, Mrs. King," she said quickly, trying to quell the panicky sense of being cornered. "I'm sure the tour guide…"

"Matteo can make the time to oblige you with his more intimate family knowledge of the park."

Intimate. A convulsive little shiver ran down Nicole's spine. Matt King literally radiated male sexuality. Even at that one brief meeting in his office she'd been sucked in by it twice, her whole body mesmerised by the attraction of his, wanting the most primitive of intimacies. She'd never felt anything so *physical.* It even messed up her mind, making it impossible to hang on to any logical thought.

"I'll call him tonight and tell him you're coming so he can watch out for you," her employer said decisively, sealing a totally unavoidable meeting.

The only question left was bus or car. Nicole didn't know which was better; trying to cling to a tour group which might diffuse Matt King's impact on her, or having her car handy so she could leave at a time of her choosing. Either way, she couldn't ignore her job which entailed gathering all the historical information she could from this trip. Somehow she would have to keep her focus on that.

"I'll go and call the tour office and see if there's a seat available on the bus," she said, rising from her chair.

Isabella Valeri King smiled her satisfaction as she nodded approval of the move. Apart from that regal nod, she didn't move herself, remaining where she sat with the quiet dignity which Nicole associated with an inner discipline that would never crack.

There was something about the smile that made her look more sharply at her rather aristocratic employer before going. She had an eerie impression of power shimmering from her...a soft but indomitable power that would not be thwarted by time or circumstance.

Again a little shiver ran down her spine.

Dark shiny eyes...almost black...like Matt's.

This family...she'd known from the beginning it wasn't ordinary...but how extraordinary was it...and where did the power come from?

She walked towards the great entrance doors to the castle, knowing she was entering their world, and finally acknowledging that running away from it wasn't really an option she wanted to take. It intrigued her. It fascinated her. Even what frightened her was also compelling.

Matt King...tomorrow.

CHAPTER FIVE

MATT stood on the balustraded roof of the pavilion café, watching the tour passengers emerge from the bus at the other end of the kauri pine avenue. Phase two of the match-making plot, he thought in amusement. Little did his grandmother know, when she'd called last night, he'd already been informed that Nicole Redman was booked to be on this bus today. He would have been waiting for her any day she chose to come.

But she hadn't chosen.

Which put a highly interesting twist on this visit. It was almost three weeks since he'd decided to keep tabs on Nicole's bus tours. She'd done almost every one of them but this, and it was clear from his conversation with his grandmother that the resident family historian had been put under pressure to come today—*his* day for this plantation.

It wouldn't have been a command. No, more a subtle manipulation, shaped in a way that undoubtedly made refusal impossible. Matt was alert to his grandmother's little tricks. But was *she* alert to the fact that Nicole Redman was very reluctant to meet him again.

What was she hiding in the cage he'd rattled?

The question had been teasing Matt's mind ever since he realised that her delay in coming here had to be de-

39

liberate. Kauri King Park was prime material for the family history. Anyone eager to research the past would have been drawn to this place within days, not weeks. So how good was Nicole Redman at the job she had taken on? How genuine? Was his grandmother being fooled? His very astute grandmother?

Unlikely, Matt decided. She might have been fooled at the beginning, but not after three weeks. Unless she was blinded by her other agenda. Was that possible? Surely she wouldn't want him to marry a con artist. She might have been beguiled by Nicole's looks, but what about character? How good an actress was this woman?

There she was! Same broad-brimmed straw hat with the sunflower. Even at this distance she stood out amongst the other tourists. She was the only woman in a skirt. The others were in shorts or light cotton slacks, teamed with loose T-shirts or skimpy tops, the usual garb for the tropics. Nicole had chosen to wear a long-sleeved blouse, the same forest green as her skirt which swung almost to her ankles.

Protecting her skin, Matt thought, but on her tall, slender figure, the effect of the outfit was very feminine. Elegantly feminine. Magnetically feminine in that crowd, especially with the hat. Others wore caps or fabric hats which were easily packed. The sunflower hat was well out of that category. It hid her hair but somehow it made an equally dramatic statement. It stood out, as everything about Nicole Redman stood out. Not one of the pack.

Matt felt his body tightening with the desire to have

her. He'd lain awake many nights, fantasising her naked on his bed, her long pale body subtly inviting him to experience every pleasure it could give him, her silky hair flaming across the pillow, a provocative promise of the fiery passion he was sure would blaze between them.

Her reluctance to meet him again had actually fuelled an urge to pursue her, but he'd restrained it, not wanting to give her any sense of power over him. Besides, there was no need to pursue when a further meeting was guaranteed, given his grandmother's game plan. Patience was the better play.

But he didn't have to be patient any longer.

She was here.

And for all she knew, he was only doing his grandmother's bidding in personally accompanying her on this tour. Which put him very neatly in control of what happened with Nicole Redman today.

Nicole stared up at the amazing kauri pines as the guide spoke about their planting, sixty years ago. They had such huge trunks running straight up to the sky, no branches at all until the very top and even the foliage they supported seemed dwarfed by the towering height of the trees. The giants of the rainforest, the guide said.

She was reminded of the giant redwoods she'd seen in Muir Woods, just outside San Francisco, but these trees were very different, a mottled bark on the trunks, not stringy, and somehow they looked more primitive. Just as majestic but...her gaze travelled slowly up the avenue as she tried to formulate her impression in words…and caught Matt King striding down it, coming straight at her.

She stood like a paralysed bunny, watching him, feeling the primitive power of him attacking her and charging every nerve in her body with a sizzling awareness of it. Her mind tried to argue he was just a man on a family mission that had been requested of him. It made no difference to his impact on her.

Her eyes registered his casual clothes, dark blue jeans and a red sports shirt. Both garments hugged his big male muscular physique, destroying any sense of security in the normality of how he was dressed. He emitted an animal-like force that could not be tamed or turned away. And the really stunning part was Nicole knew it excited her. Something uncontrollable inside her was wildly thrilled by it.

"Good morning," he called to her while he was still some metres away.

Even his voice seemed to put an extra thrum in her bloodstream. She took a deep breath as she fiercely willed herself to respond in a natural fashion. The purpose of her visit here was to see and understand what had been achieved with this park, and the exotic fruit plantation beyond it.

"Hello," she said, more awkwardly than she would have liked. "It's good of you to come and greet me but please…if you should be doing something else…"

He grinned, his dark eyes twinkling at her obvious discomfort. "I don't mind obliging my grandmother, adding my bit to the history of this place."

"The tour…"

"Has moved on while you waited for me."

The realisation he spoke the truth brought an instant flush of embarrassment. She hadn't even noticed, hadn't heard the guide directing everyone elsewhere, hadn't been aware she'd been left standing alone. A babble of voices drew her gaze to the left-hand side of the kauri pine avenue. The group had been diverted down a path bordered by electric-blue ferns.

"Shall we follow or…?"

"Yes," she quickly decided, choosing the safety of numbers and hopefully a dilution of the effect Matt King had on her.

She started off after them and he fell into step beside her, making her extremely conscious of how tall he was. She was above average height for a woman but she was only on eye level with his shoulder, and walking side by side, the broad brim of her hat was a barrier to looking directly at him and vice versa, which gave her time to regain some composure.

"So how's it all going for you?" he asked, reminding her of his sceptical view of her staying power at the castle with his grandmother.

"Fine!" she answered lightly.

"Not feeling swamped?"

"By what?"

"By all the information you'll have to fit into a coherent story."

"It's a big story. Big in every sense. But not overwhelming. There's an innate order to it."

"As there is to any life," he dryly commented. "I assume there's a logic to yours."

"Yes, I guess there is. Though I haven't really reflected on it in that light."

"Perhaps you prefer a haphazard pattern."

"I don't think so."

"But you *are* willing to take on new experiences, despite obvious drawbacks. You're committed to being in Port Douglas for six months although the climate here can't be kind to you."

He was digging at her again, just as he had in his office. Why did he want her to admit she'd made a mistake in taking on this project? Was she some kind of thorn in his side?

"I think it's a wonderful climate," she asserted with a sense of perverse satisfaction in flouting his opinion. "No cold," she added pointedly. "I hate the cold."

"You don't find the heat oppressive?"

"It can be if I'm outside in the middle of the day," she conceded.

"Particularly when you have to cover up to protect your fair skin."

"I'm done that all my life. It doesn't bother me."

"Well, you don't need your hat on now. We're in total shade. And I prefer not to talk to a straw brim."

She had a stubborn impulse to deny him her bare face. On the other hand, he might have the gall to lift her hat off himself, just as he'd taken the liberty of putting it on her head in his office. Better to avoid that kind of familiar contact. She was barely hanging on to a semblance of control as it was. Besides which, it was true the rainforest canopy had now blocked out the sun. It was unreasonable and probably offensive to stick to wearing the hat so she reached up and removed it.

"There! Doesn't that feel better?"

She looked up into wickedly teasing eyes and the strong impression thumped into her heart that he would very much enjoy stripping her of all her coverings. It triggered the thought that he was as sexually attracted to her as she was to him. Which completely blew her mind.

Instinctively she sought time out by attaching herself to the tour group and focusing fiercely on the official guide who was naming ferns and vines. It reminded her she should be paying attention, taking notes, keeping an eye out for what might make good photographs to illustrate what had been achieved here. Determined to get on with her job and not let *this thing* with Matt King throw her completely off course, she fumbled in her carry-bag for her notebook and biro...and dropped her hat.

In a trice Matt scooped it up. "I'll carry it for you."

Heat whooshed into her cheeks. She just knew he'd put it back on her head himself when they emerged into sunshine and he'd reduce her to a quivering mess of jangling nerve-ends. "Thanks," she mumbled, wishing she hadn't clipped back her hair, wishing it was veiling her face as she hunted in her bag for the elusive objects. "I do need my hands free to take notes," she added, finally producing the evidence of this intention, taking out her camera, as well, and hanging it around her neck for easy access.

He reached out, slid his hand around the nape of her neck and lifted her hair out from under the camera strap. Nicole stood stock-still, her heart hammering, her face burning. "Just freeing your hair," he excused, but his fingers stroked down its length before he dropped the uninvited contact.

She didn't know what to do. She'd never felt like this before, so super-conscious of touch, of *who* was touching and the shivery intimacy of it, *the wanting* she could feel lingering on her skin and her own physical response so vibrant it swallowed up any possibility of making even a token protest.

She found herself gripping the notebook and biro with knuckle-white intensity and tried to concentrate on hearing what the guide was saying, jotting down snatches of words which would probably never make sense to her later. It simply gave her some purpose beyond being aware of Matt King beside her, Matt King watching her. Her mind shied from thinking about what he was thinking.

Maybe her imagination was running riot anyway. Let him speak, she decided. If he truly was interested in her as a woman, let him spell that out in no uncertain terms so no mistake could be made on her side. If he didn't, she could conclude that attraction was one thing, pursuing it quite another. He might very well think a relationship with her could end up with more problems than pleasure.

The last thing she wanted was to make a fool of herself over her employer's grandson. It would put her in a dreadfully embarrassing position with no easy escape from it. She had to stay at the castle for five more months and in that length of time there would undoubtedly be family occasions involving him. Caution had to be maintained here. Her own pride and self-respect demanded it. Yet the desire for some verbal rapport with him kept her very much on edge, waiting, listening.

To her intense frustration, Matt King said nothing out of the ordinary. He simply adopted the role of casual companion. They strolled along at the tail end of the tour group, stopping when the group stopped, looking at whatever was being pointed out to them. Nicole took photographs when others were taking photographs, regardless of whether they might be usable for the project or not. It used up otherwise idle time—time which might have led into dangerous ground with Matt King.

As it was, he commented on her prolific use of the camera. "Are these photos for your own private pleasure of do you imagine they'll provide some kind of pictorial history?" he said with a mocking amusement that needled her into justifying the activity.

"I don't know yet what will best illustrate this place when I come to writing about it. It will be good to have all these shots to choose from."

One black eyebrow arched quizzically. "Have you done much writing so far?"

"I'm still taking notes."

"So I see."

The dry tone and a flash of scepticism in his eyes implied he doubted she would ever get around to serious writing. It ruffled Nicole's feathers on a professional level. He had no right to judge her ability to produce what was required. Though she had to concede her erratic note-taking today might not have impressed him.

"I think you'll find the photographs in my home of more pertinent interest—historically speaking—than any you've taken today," he drawled. "They show stages of the park from its inception to its completed state."

"Why didn't you tell me before?"

"Oh, it was interesting observing what you thought was important. Besides which, you could have asked me." He slanted her a sardonic smile. "I didn't really make myself available to you just to carry your hat."

Nicole could have died on the spot. She'd been so flustered by his physical presence, so caught up in her own response to it, she hadn't *used* him as she should have done as a source of information on this part of the family history.

"I'm sorry. I was so carried away by the park as it is now…" She shook her head in obvious self-chiding and managed an apologetic grimace. "You must think I'm some kind of fraud."

It was a toss-off line, one she expected him to deny, letting her off the hook. Instead, he delivered another blow to her self-esteem.

"Are you?"

She stopped, shocked that he could actually be thinking that. Her gaze whipped up to his and found his dark eyes glittering with a very sharp intensity.

"No, I'm not," she stated with considerable heat.

He cocked his head assessingly. "Then is there some reason you must cling to this public tour?"

"I...I came with it."

"And I'll see you return to it before it leaves. Failing that, I'll drive you back to Port Douglas myself."

Her heart was catapulting around her chest at the thought of spending the next few hours alone with Matt King. She could feel the force of his will pressing on her, commanding surrender, and once again feeling under attack, she struggled to retain her independence from him.

"We're heading for the pavilion now," she rushed out. "I'd like to walk around it."

"Of course." A taunting little smile curved his lips as he waved her into trailing after the group again. "It was built as a recreation centre for the internees. It gives a fine focal point to the kauri pine avenue and it overlooks the tennis courts on the other side. People can sit on the roof of the pavilion and watch tournaments being played."

"And your great-grandfather designed it all," Nicole quickly slipped in to show her mind *was* on family history.

"Yes. No doubt you've already noticed the touch of old Rome in the construction of the building," he returned dryly.

The central block was surrounded by colonnades and the balustrade enclosing the flat roof was cast in a Roman style. "All that's missing is a fountain," she commented.

He laughed. "There's a row of fountains in a long rectangular pond on the other side." He grinned at her. "Nothing was missed. Frederico Stefano Valeri was very thorough in everything he took on."

Impulse spilled the question, "Are you?"

His eyes danced teasingly. "I guess history will be the judge of that."

"The tour carries on to your exotic fruit plantation after refreshments in the pavilion."

"Just feeding a curiosity. You can pick up all the information you might need on that from the pamphlets in the pavilion. You won't miss anything important." Again he grinned. "A detour to my home will save you a long walk in the heat."

There really was no choice but to go with him. Trying to postpone it longer than she already had would only feed his suspicions she was not up to the job she'd been employed to do. She could hardly explain that *he* was the problem.

"I'll even give you a personal sampling of the exotic fruit I grow," he added, piling on the pressure. "Along with any other refreshment you'd like."

Sheer wickedness in his eyes.

He knew she didn't want to accompany him.

He was playing a game with her—trap Nicole Redman.

But for what purpose?

Was he about to get…very personal…once they were alone together?

Her pulse drummed in her temples. Her whole body

was seized with a chaotically wanton urge to experience this man, but she didn't trust it to lead anywhere good. The sexual pull was very strong—very, very strong— yet other instincts were screaming something was wrong about Matt King's game.

And that meant she had to stay alert and somehow keep a safety door open so she could walk out of the trap with her personal integrity intact.

CHAPTER SIX

DESPITE Matt King's unnerving company, Nicole loved his house. He ushered her into a large open living area which was instantly inviting, full of colour and casual comfort. The floor was of blue-green slate, cool underfoot. The room was cool, too, no doubt kept that way by an air-conditioner—blissful relief from the late-morning heat.

At one side, three green leather chesterfields formed a U to face a huge television screen. A long wooden table with eight chairs balanced it on the other side. A kitchen with a big island bench was accessible to both areas, and beyond them a wall of glass led out to a veranda.

Other walls held paintings of the rainforest and scenes of the Great Barrier Reef with its fabulous coral and tropical fish. It was very clear Matt King loved his environment and was very much at home in it. Even the outside of the house was painted green to merge with its surroundings and the approach to it was beautifully landscaped with palms and shrubs exhibiting exotic flowers or foliage.

"I'll get some refreshments," Matt said, heading into the kitchen. "Leave your things on the table and go on out to the veranda. It overhangs a creek so you'll find it cool enough. Nice place to relax with the sound of water adding to the view.''

Any place she could relax was a good idea, Nicole thought, following Matt's instructions. At least he had given her back her hat to put on herself, and he wasn't crowding her now as she took it off again and set it on the table with her bag. Maybe it was stupid to feel so tense. Directing her onto his veranda surely indicated he was not about to pounce on her.

A sliding-glass door led onto it and Nicole moved straight over to the railing, drawn by the sound of rushing water. The creek below ran over clumps of boulders in a series of small cascades. It sparkled with a crystal-like clarity and the view was so pretty with the banks covered with ferns, she momentarily forgot all her troubles.

Birds flitted amongst the trees, their calls adding a special music to the scene—soft warbles, sharp staccatos, tinkling trills. She caught glimpses of beautiful plumage; gold, purple, scarlet. This was a magical place and she thought how lucky Matt King was that he could lay claim to it. To live here with all this...the sheer natural beauty of it, the tranquility...absolute Eden.

''Don't move,'' came the quietly voiced command from behind her. ''Butterflies have landed on your hair. Just let them be until I get a flower and move them off.''

She stood very still, entranced by the idea of butterflies being drawn to her, not frightened by her foreign presence. There was the sound of a tray being set on a table, Matt's footsteps as he walked to the end of the veranda and returned. Out of the corner of her eye she glimpsed a bright red hibiscus bloom in his hand, a long yellow stamen at its centre. She felt a light brushing on her hair, then suddenly two vivid blue butterflies were fluttering in front of her, poised over the flower which Matt was now holding out over the railing.

"Oh!" she breathed in sheer wonder. "What a brilliant blue they are!"

"Ulysses butterflies. Lots of them around here," Matt murmured. "The bright colour of your hair attracted them."

"Really?" She looked at him in surprise, still captivated by the pleasure of the experience.

He smiled, even with his eyes, and he was standing so close, it was like being bathed in tingling warmth. For a few heart-lifting moments, it seemed they shared the same vision of the marvels of nature, felt the same appreciation. Then the warmth simmered to a far less comfortable level and Nicole could feel herself tensing again.

"Drawn to the flame," he said in a soft musing tone that set her skin prickling. "I wonder how many it has consumed?"

"I beg your pardon?" she said stiffly.

"Moths…men…your hair is a magnet."

"It doesn't consume things."

"It has the allure of a *femme fatale*."

"I don't see you falling at my feet."

He laughed and teasingly drew the soft petals of the hibiscus flower down her cheek. It was a shockingly sensual action and he enjoyed every second of it while she lost the ability to breathe, let alone speak.

"Life is full of surprises," he said enigmatically. "Let me surprise your tastebuds with many exotic flavours."

He stepped back and gestured to the table where he'd left the tray. It was a table for two, cane with a glass top, and two cane chairs with green cushions on their seats stood waiting for them. The tray held a platter containing an array of sliced fruit, two small plates with knives and forks and two elegant flute glasses filled with what looked like...

"Champagne?" The word slipped out, bringing home to Nicole how far out of control she was.

"The best complement for the fruit," Matt said with an authority that seemed to make protesting the alcoholic drink too mean-spirited to try. He smiled encouragingly. "It's chilled, which I'm sure you'll appreciate."

He was waiting for her to take her chair. Nicole took a deep breath, needing to collect her scattered wits, and pushed her jelly-like legs into action. As she seated herself, Matt unloaded the tray and placed the scarlet hibiscus flower beside her glass of champagne, a taunting reminder of how easily she could lose her head with this man. She vowed to sip the champagne sparingly.

He sat down and grinned at her, anticipation of pleasure dancing in his eyes, making her heart contract with the thought that it was not the prospect of eating fruit exhilarating him. She was the target and he was lining her up for the kill. Although her mind was hopelessly woolly on what *kill* meant.

"I think we should start with what is commonly re-garded as the king and queen of all tropical fruit." He forked two pieces of fruit onto her plate, pointing each one out as he named them. "The king is durian. The queen is mangosteen."

The durian was similar to a custard apple, only much richer in flavour. Nicole preferred the more delicate taste of the sweet-acid segment of mangosteen. "I like the queen better," she declared.

"Perhaps the king is more of an acquired taste. The more you eat it the more addictive it becomes."

Was he subtly promising this about himself?

"Now here we have the black sapote. It's like choc-olate pudding."

He watched her taste it, making her acutely conscious of her mouth and the sensual pleasure of the fruit.

"You'll need to clean your palate after that one," he advised, picking up his glass of champagne and nodding to hers.

She followed suit as he sipped, her own gaze drawn to his mouth, wondering what it would taste like if he kissed her.

"Try a longan. It's originally from China and similar to a lychee."

So it went on—exotic names, exotic tastes—but more and more Nicole was thinking erotic, not exotic. There was a very sexy intimacy in sharing this feast of oral sensations, the conscious sorting out of flavours on the tongue, mouths moving in matching action, relishing de-licious juices, trying to define interesting textures, watching each other's response, the telling expressions to each different experience...like an exciting journey of discovery...exciting on many levels.

Matt King...he stirred needs and desires in her that wanted answering. He embodied so much of all she had missed out on in her own life and the craving to know if he could fill that emptiness was growing stronger and stronger. It wasn't just that he was the sexiest man she'd ever met. It felt like...he was a complete person...and she wasn't.

Perhaps it had to do with having a firm foundation of family, a sense of roots, a clear continuity. She felt she was still looking for *her place,* both in a physical and spiritual sense. She wished this was her home, wished she could belong here, wished Matt King would invite her into more of his world.

"Would you like some more champagne?"

It jolted her into the realisation that she'd drained her glass without even noticing the fact. "No," she said quickly. "It was lovely, thank you. It's all been lovely...the park, your home, the fruit, sitting out here with this wonderful view..."

"And you haven't even minded my company," he slid in, his eyes telegraphing the certain knowledge of what had been shared in the past half hour.

Nicole shied from acknowledging too much, telling herself she still had to be careful of consequences. "You've been very generous."

"A pleasure." His smile seemed to mock her caution. "Would you like to see the photographs now?"

"Yes, please."

He laughed as he rose from his chair. "You sound like a little girl. Which makes me wonder how full of contradictions you are, Nicole Redman."

"I'm not aware of any," she retorted lightly, standing to accompany him.

"You're very definitely a tantalising mix." He slanted her a mocking look as he ushered her back into the house. "I'd find it interesting to delve into your history, but that's not why you're here, is it?"

"No." What else could she say? This wasn't a *social* visit. But if he really wanted to know more about her...or was he testing her again? Challenging her? Why did he make her feel uneasy about what should be straightforward?

They walked through the living room. At one end of the kitchen he opened a door which led into a very workman-like office. The far wall had a picture window with a spectacular view of the rainforest park. A long L-shaped desk held a computer, printer, fax machine, telephone, photocopier—all the modern equipment necessary for running a home business. File cabinets lined the other wall. Above them was a series of large framed photographs, depicting various stages of the park.

Nicole was instantly fascinated by them. Matt drew her attention to a framed drawing above the printer. "You should look at this first. It's the original plan, sketched by my great-grandfather. This is what the internees worked from."

It was amazing...the thought, the detail, the vision of the man. "Do you have a photocopy of this?"

"Yes, I can give you one. Now if you look over here..." He directed her to the first photograph by the door. "The first thing planted was this fast-growing bamboo, all around the perimeter of the camp to block out the fences which represented emprisonment."

Understanding and caring, Nicole thought, again marvelling at what a remarkable person Frederico Stefano Valeri had been. As they moved from one photograph to the next, with Matt explaining the story behind each stage of the park, giving it all a very human purpose, she couldn't help wondering if goodness was inherited, as well as strength and the will to meet and beat any adversity.

There was no doubting the strength, both physical and mental, in the man beside her, but what was in Matt King's heart? Was it as big as his great-grandfather's? Did it hold kindness, tenderness? What moved him to act? Would he stand up for others?

Most people, Nicole reflected, were little people, wrapped up in their own self-interest. They didn't stride through life, shaping it in new ways for the benefit of others. Yet from all she'd learnt of the Valeri/King family, they did just that, certainly profiting themselves, but never at the cost of others. They were *big* people, in every sense.

Her gaze was drawn to the muscular arm pointing to the last photograph, tanned skin gleaming over tensile strength. Her own skin looked white next to his, white and soft, unweathered by time or place. Perhaps it was the contrast that made him so compellingly attractive.

His arm dropped.

The deep rich timbre of his voice was no longer thrumming in her ears.

She looked up to find him observing her with heart-squeezing intensity. Having completely lost track of what he'd been saying, she held her tongue rather than make some embarrassing *faux pas*.

"I have the original photos filed if you want to make use of them," he said, but she knew intuitively that wasn't on his mind.

She shook her head. "I'd rather not have the originals. They're precious. If you could have copies made for me…"

"As you like. I'll bring them to the castle when they're done."

"Thank you."

"It *is* too much for you, isn't it?"

"What?"

"It would be fairer to my grandmother if you admit it now."

"I don't know what you mean."

"Do I have to shake it out of you?" His hands closed around her upper arms, giving substance to the threat.

Alarm screeched around her nerves. "I think you've got something terribly wrong here. Please let me go."

He released her, throwing up his hands in a gesture of angry impatience. His eyes blazed with accusation. "You might have been able to swan through God knows what else on your looks and your ability to adopt a role convincingly, but let me tell you your performance on this project today has been too damned shallow for me to swallow.''

"It's your fault!'' she hurled back at him. "Making me nervous and…''

"And why do you suppose that is, Nicole?'' he savagely mocked. "Because I recognise you for what you are?''

She stepped back, confused by the violence of feeling coming from him. It was like a body blow, shattering any possible sense of togetherness with him, shrivelling the desire he'd aroused in her.

"What am I…to you?'' she asked, needing some reason for this attack.

His mouth curled sardonically. "The same bewitching woman I watched in New Orleans ten years ago.''

"New Orleans?'' He was there…when she was there with her father?

"Don't tell me it's some mistake. The image of you is burned on my memory. Indelibly.''

"I don't remember you.''

"You wouldn't. I was masked that night.''

"What night?''

"You must have spent many nights spinning your ghostly tales on the haunted history tour. You were very good at it.''

"Yes, I was.'' Her chin lifted with defiant pride. "So what? That was ten years ago.'' And she wasn't ashamed of raking in the tourist dollar then, any more than he'd be of doing it now.

A black cynicism glittered in his eyes. "Still spinning tales, Nicole? Drawing people in? Getting them to shell out money with clever fabrications and exaggerations? Pulling the wool over their eyes? Eyes already dazzled by the striking combination of pearly skin and flame-red hair?"

Shock spilled into outrage at his interpretation of her character. He had no cause at all to think she was some kind of confidence trickster. Even if she had embellished those old tales a bit, it was only to add to the fun of the tour, giving people more for their money.

"I was doing a job," she cried emphatically. "The only job I could get at the time. I followed a script I was given. I certainly didn't fleece anyone. Everyone got good value on the haunted history."

"And now you're fully qualified to research and write a family history." Scepticism laced every word. "Except you haven't quite demonstrated a fine nose for it today."

"You're right!" she snapped, feeling more and more brittle. "I'm much better at it when there's no hostile force muddling my mind."

"Hostile?" he derided. "I gave you every chance to prove you were on top of this job. You even lost track of what I was telling you right here."

"I was thinking."

"Sure you were! And maybe you were thinking what I was thinking..." His eyes raked her from head to foot and up again. "…how well we might go together in bed."

Her skin was burning. Her insides were quivering. She was in a total mess. For a few soul-destroying seconds she stared at him, knowing at least she hadn't been wrong about the mutual sexual attraction but there was nothing to feel good about in that. No way in the world could she stomach any physical intimacy with him now.

"Please excuse me," she said with icy dignity. "I'll go and rejoin the tour."

A fierce pride gave her the power to walk out of his office and cross the living area to the table where she'd left her hat and bag. She was shaking as she picked them up.

"Running away won't resolve anything."

The mocking drawl flicked her on the raw. She turned her head to give him one last blistering look. He was leaning against the doorjamb, the loose-limbed pose denying any tension on his part. An ironic little smile played on his lips.

"Better to face up to the situation and try to make it more workable," he advised. "I could get you some help."

Her jaw clenched at this offer. She managed to unclench it enough to say, "Provided I satisfy you in bed?"

That wiped the smile off his face. "I don't trade in sexual favours, Nicole."

"Neither do I. And I've always found prejudice quite impossible for resolving anything. Please check my professional credentials with your grandmother before we have to meet again. I'd prefer not to feel under fire from you in future.''

She didn't run, but she swept out of his house as fast as she could at a walking pace. He didn't come after her, for which she was intensely grateful because she was right on the edge of bursting into tears. Anger, frustration, disappointment…all of them were churning through her, and she hated herself for having given him any reason to think what he did.

She would not be vulnerable to his…his aggressive maleness…ever again.

Just let him come near her.

Just let him.

She would freeze him into eternity!

CHAPTER SEVEN

THREE hours, Matt told himself, as he drove to the Sunday luncheon he couldn't avoid. Four at most. He should easily manage to pass that length of time with his family without putting a foot wrong with Nicole Redman. He could do a show of polite interest in her work, enough to satisfy his grandmother's standard of good manners, and spend the rest of the time chatting to his brothers.

He was not about to make any judgments today. Let Nicole Redman stew in her inadequacies as far as the family history was concerned. He'd brought the photographs and the photocopied plan she'd requested. He'd hand them over to her and that was his bit done. She wasn't about to seek him out for anything more and be damned if he'd chase her for anything, either.

What was it…ten days since he'd called her bluff? The gall of her to blame *him* for *her* lack of professionalism on the project! Sheer amateursville taking all those tourist photos in the park. No theme, no purpose, just click, click, click. And calling him a hostile force…huh! She hadn't thought he was hostile while they shared the fruit platter on the veranda.

A pity he hadn't taken his chance then and there.

It was well and truly gone now.

Though it was better he hadn't got sexually involved with her. She probably cheated on that level, too, promising more than she'd ever deliver. Visual pleasure definitely wasn't everything. And reality rarely lived up to fantasy.

His grandmother could have Nicole Redman all to herself from now on. She would just have to accept that her matchmaking scheme had bombed out and live with the consequences of her choice. It wasn't paramount that the family history be published at the end of Nicole's contract. Another person could be brought in to get it right. This was not a full-scale disaster, more a minor mess they could all sweep under the carpet.

On the marriage front, she had ready consolation for her disappointment with him. This luncheon…Tony's pressure for him to be there…reading between the lines, Tony was bursting to celebrate with the family the fact that he and Hannah were expecting their first baby. Had to be. Hannah wanted a whole pack of children, having come from a big family herself, and Tony had declared himself happy to oblige her. Three months married…time enough for Hannah to get pregnant.

So today was bound to be happy families day for Nonna. She'd have Alex's and Gina's two children to cluck over and Tony and Hannah promising another great-grandchild. Plenty of good stuff for her to focus on. She could count her blessings and forget about him for a while. A *long* while. He'd get married in his own good time to his own choice of wife.

He drove in to the private parking area behind the

castle, noting that Alex's Mercedes was already there and Tony's helicopter was sitting on the pad. He was the last to arrive, which was good. Easier to lose Nicole Redman in a crowd, although if his grandmother parked him with her at the dining table... Matt gritted his teeth, knowing he couldn't completely ignore her. He hated being boxed into a corner. Hated it!

Using the back entrance, he strode along to the kitchen where he was bound to find Rosita, who knew everything there was to know about what went on in the castle. She'd not only been the cook and housekeeper here for over twenty years, she was his grandmother's closest confidante, sharing the same Italian heritage and always sympathetic to her plans.

She was at the island bench, tasting a salad with an air of testing its ingredients for the correct balance. Matt grinned at her. Rosita loved food and didn't mind being plump because of it. He and his brothers had been fed many great feasts in this kitchen.

"Have you got it right?" he teased.

"This is Hannah's special salad. An interesting combination...cabbage, noodles, walnuts...but you do not want to know these things." She gestured expansively. "It is good to see you, Matteo!"

"You, too, Rosita." He gave her a quick hug. "How's everything going here?"

"Oh, busy, busy, busy. You will find everyone in the billiard room."

That surprised him. "Why the billiard room?" He couldn't imagine Alex and Tony wanting to play today.

"It is where Nicole has her work on the family history. Your grandmother is showing them what's been done so far.''

''Well, that should be interesting,'' Matt said dryly, wondering how Nicole was managing to convince them that anything had been done.

''She works too hard, that girl.'' Rosita shook her head disapprovingly. ''Up all hours of the night. I make a supper for her but more times than not she forgets to eat.''

''Definitely a crime,'' Matt commented with mock gravity.

''Oh, go on with you!'' She shooed him away. ''And do not leave it so long again before visiting your grandmother. Over a month.''

''Busy, busy, busy,'' he tossed back as he left the kitchen.

''Young people,'' he heard her mutter disparagingly. ''Rush, rush, rush.''

But Matt didn't *rush* to the billiard room. He was considerably bemused by the picture painted of Nicole Redman by Rosita. Hardworking? And why was such a large room being taken up for this project? How did she justify it?

The door was open. The rest of the family didn't even notice his arrival. Their attention was fixed on the billiard table which was still wearing its protective cover. A quick sweeping glance told Matt Nicole Redman was not present, which made his greeting much more relaxed.

''Hi!'' he said, strolling forward. ''What's the big deal here?''

Everyone answered at once, saying hello and urging him into their midst to look at what was fascinating them. The surface of the billiard table held a pictorial history of the family, a massed display of old photographs, arranged in sequential decades, with a typed annotation of who, where and why underneath each one. Some of them Matt had never seen, or if he had, he didn't remember them.

"This is great, Nonna," he couldn't help remarking.

"Nicole and I have been sorting them for weeks. These are the best from a store of old albums and boxes."

Probably more his grandmother's work than Nicole's, Matt decided.

"Have a look at this time line, Matt." Tony waved him over to a whiteboard which he was now studying. "All the big dates lined up—the wars, the mafia interference, the cyclones, the whole progress of the sugar industry, when the other plantations became viable…and on this side of the line, notes on what the family was doing through these critical times. Just the bare bones but it gets the history in perspective, doesn't it?"

It did. In fact, Matt had to concede it was quite an impressive summary. And a very logical method of getting the whole story in order. He was beginning to have a nasty niggly feeling he might have misjudged Nicole Redman. Yet if she really could do this job, why had she been so inept during her visit to Kauri King Park?

Which reminded him of the bag he was carrying. He turned to his grandmother. "I've got more photographs here. Shots of the park being built. Nicole asked me to get copies of the originals and a photocopy of the plan. Where should I put them?"

"On her desk. Thank you, Matteo."

Following the direction of his grandmother's nod, Matt saw that a large desk had been brought in and positioned under the window at the far end of the room. It held a laptop computer, piles of manila folders, a tape-player and a stack of cassettes which Alex was sorting through, picking up each cassette and reading the label.

"So what's Nicole Redman's taste in music?" Matt asked as he put the bag next to the computer.

"It's not music. They're interviews with the old families in the Italian community. Nonna said she's off doing another one today."

"Not joining us for lunch then?" Matt now had mixed feelings about whether he wanted her there or not. Easier for him if she wasn't, but if he was guilty of prejudice— and the evidence was stacking up against the assumptions he'd made—an apology was due.

"No. She's gone down to the Johnstone Shire. A couple of hours' drive. Won't be back until late afternoon, I should think."

Free of her.

Except she sat uncomfortably on his conscience.

"She's certainly compiled a lot of material this past month," Alex remarked admiringly.

"Yes, but can she write?" Matt snapped, part of him needing to justify his stance with her.

Alex gave him a startled look. "Don't you know…?" He stopped, frowned. "That's right. You weren't at the lunch when Nonna introduced Nicole to the rest of us. One of the reasons Nonna chose her to do this was the biography she'd written of her father."

"A biography," Matt repeated, stunned by this new information.

"Mmm... It's called *Ollie's Drum*. Her father was a jazz musician."

Jazz... New Orleans...

"Have *you* read it?" he shot at his oldest brother, whose opinion he'd always respected.

"No." Alex gave him a droll look. "But biographies don't get published unless the author can write, Matt. Besides, Nonna has read it and it satisfied her."

Ollie's Drum. Matt fixed the title in his mind. He needed to get hold of that book, read it for himself. The ferocity of that thought gave him pause to examine it more rationally. What was the point of pursuing more information about her? If he'd blotted his copybook with Nicole Redman, so what? Hadn't he already decided any kind of relationship with her was not on?

Though he didn't like feeling he hadn't been fair.

Injustice of any kind was anathema to him.

On the other hand, she'd given him every reason to think what he had, and accusing him of being a hostile force, making her nervous...absolute hogwash!

"You're right off base if you're thinking Nicole Redman isn't up to this job," Alex remarked, eyeing him curiously.

"I didn't say that."

An eyebrow was cocked, challenging any doubt at all. "She's got a swag of degrees. History, genealogy, literature..."

Degrees could be forged. With today's computers almost anything could be made to look genuine.

"She's taught various courses at a tafe college, too," Alex went on. "Very highly qualified. Nonna was lucky to get her."

Not even a hint of suspicion that Nicole was not as she had presented herself. If Alex was sold on her...and Alex certainly didn't have a matchmaking agenda...then it had to be conceded Nicole did have the ability to do this job.

Which meant he should apologise.

The sooner, the better, in fact. She couldn't be feeling good about a member of the family casting aspersions on her integrity. She might very well have gone out today to avoid the unpleasantness of his presence. And working on a Sunday could be taken as a slap in the face to him for doubting her commitment to the project.

Her absence suddenly felt very personal.

Matt didn't like it one bit. He'd never been painted as a hostile ogre before. He wished he hadn't brought up the sexual angle with her. It made the situation doubly awkward when it came to back-pedalling on the stance he'd taken. Nevertheless, he couldn't just walk away from it. She had another five months left on this project and leaving her under a black cloud where he was concerned, was not right.

This *blot* had to be confronted and dealt with.

Today.

Even if he had to wait hours for her to return to the castle.

CHAPTER EIGHT

NICOLE glanced at her watch as she drove into the castle grounds, heading for the family parking area at the back. Almost five o'clock. Late enough for everyone to have gone home. Not that she would have minded saying hello to Matt King's older brothers and she really liked their wives. Gina was genuinely warm-hearted and Hannah literally bubbled with the joy of life. Probably more so now if she was expecting a baby, as Mrs. King suspected.

No doubt she would hear all the family news over dinner tonight, though it was a shame she had missed out on Hannah's excitement. Nicole instantly argued that Matt King's presence at the luncheon would have dampened it for her anyway. And if he'd been seated next to her at the dining table...she shuddered at the thought. An utterly intolerable situation.

It was reassuring to see that the helipad was empty. Clearly Tony and Hannah had flown back to their home on the tea plantation at Cape Tribulation. Alex's Mercedes was not in the parking lot, but the one car sitting by itself gave Nicole's heart a nasty lurch—a forest-green Saab convertible, a typical choice for a wealthy, sexy bachelor like Matt King.

She brought her own modest little Toyota to a halt

beside it and sat, fighting a sickening rise of tension. She couldn't be certain the sporty convertible was his since she'd never seen him driving a vehicle. Nevertheless, any hope that it belonged to someone else didn't feel very feasible.

Best to assume he had stayed behind with his grandmother and stay clear of where they might be. If she could scoot upstairs to the privacy of her bedroom…no, that would mean passing the library. Maybe she could slink into the billiard room without being seen.

Nicole thumped the driving wheel in disgust at these *fugitive* thoughts. Why should she let herself be intimidated by Matt King? It was wrong. *He* was wrong. While she certainly didn't want to meet him again, it was absurd to shrink from doing so when she was absolutely entitled to hold her ground.

Determined on acting normally, she alighted from her car and walked into the castle, intent on heading openly to the billiard room where she would take her briefcase and empty it of the material collected today. This meant passing through the kitchen and predictably Rosita was there. It was a considerable relief to find the motherly housekeeper alone.

''Ah! You are back!'' she said in a satisfied tone, as though Nicole was some recalcitrant chick who had finally returned to the nest.

''Yes, I'm back. Is Hannah expecting a baby, Rosita?''

A triumphant clap of the hands. ''Two months pregnant! It is very happy news.''

"How lovely!"

"And Matteo is still here, talking to his grandmother. If you would like to go on out to the loggia and join them, I will bring some fresh drinks."

"I'd rather let them enjoy each other's company, Rosita," she quickly excused. "I have some work to get into my computer while it's still fresh in my mind."

This announcement earned a disapproving tut but Nicole was off before Rosita could gear up for her argument that there was more to life than work, especially for a young woman who had not yet been fortunate enough to find a husband to take care of her.

As Nicole walked down the hall to the billiard room, she darkly decided that if Rosita was fondly casting her employer's third grandson in that role, she was doomed to disappointment. No way was matrimonial bliss on that horizon!

In fact, the thought of joining Matt King in any sense raised hackles that might have drawn blood had she gone out to the loggia, despite her respect for her employer. She closed the door of the billiard room very firmly behind her, willing her antagonist to keep his distance because she was not prepared to suffer any more slights on her integrity.

And if he had checked out her qualifications today, she hoped he was stewing in guilt over his rotten accusations. Not that it was likely. He was too arrogantly sure of himself to think he might have been mistaken. Just because he'd been right about the sexual attraction... Nicole heaved a big sigh to relieve the mounting anger in her chest as she marched over to her desk.

Enough was enough!

How many nights had she lain awake, seething over their last encounter? It was such a foolish waste of time and energy. The man was not worth thinking about. To let him get under her skin as far as he had was just plain stupid.

She switched on the computer with more force than was needed. Work was the answer to blocking out unpleasant connections from her consciousness. Her gaze fell on a bag that didn't belong on her desk. A long cardboard cylinder protruded from it. Frowning over the Kauri Pine Park logo on the bag, she set her briefcase on the floor, uncomfortably aware that she had asked Matt King for copies of photographs and the original plan of the park. Was this his delivery?

Her hands clenched, not wanting to touch anything he had touched. Had he brought this bag in here himself, invading her private space, spying on what work she'd done? She shot a quick glance around the room, looking for anything out of place. Only the bag. Yet somehow the very air felt charged with his presence.

It was unnerving, inhibiting. She stared at the bag, telling herself its contents were completely harmless. It didn't matter if they were meant to mock her position here at the castle. She would use them effectively and show Matt King how very professional she was. Even if he never backed down from his insulting judgment of her, she'd know that he had to know he was wrong once the history was published. There could be no refuting that evidence. In the end, she would triumph.

The only problem was…it didn't take away the hurt.

A knock on the door sent wild tremors through her heart. *Not him…please…not him,* her mind begged as she heard the door open.

"Nicole?"

His voice.

She wanted to keep her back turned to him but what good would that do? *He* would have no compunction about walking in and doing whatever he wanted. She could feel his forceful energy hitting her, commanding an acknowledgment of him. If he didn't get it, he would engineer a confrontation one way or another.

"May I come in?"

The polite query cut into the fierce flow of resentment in her mind. It was just a sham of good manners, she swiftly told herself. The predatory nature of the man simply would not accept a negative reply. Nevertheless, pride in her own good manners demanded he be faced and answered.

Instinctively she squared her shoulders, stiffened her spine, armouring herself against his impact. Impossible to calm her heart. She half turned, enough to see him, watch him, while giving him the least possible target to fire at.

"What do you want?" Blunt words, but she didn't care. Why wait for his attack? Better to get it over with quickly.

He closed the door behind him, ensuring privacy. His

face wore a grimly determined look, causing Nicole's stomach to contract in apprehension. The sense of his presence was now magnified a hundredfold. She forced her gaze to rake him from head to toe, as he had done to her at their last meeting, but there was no sexual intent behind the action, more a need to reduce him to just a body without the power behind his eyes.

Except it wasn't just a body.

It had power, too.

And it struck her as hopelessly perverse that she could still feel attracted to it, everything that was female in her responding with treacherous excitement to the aggressive masculinity of his perfectly sculpted physique.

"I want to apologise."

The words wafted quietly across the room and slid soothingly into ears that were clogged by the clamouring of her heart. Nicole wondered if she had imagined them. She saw his hands lift in an open gesture of appeal, giving some credibility to what she'd heard. Her gaze lifted to his mouth, waiting for it to move, to say more, to mitigate the deep offence he'd given.

"I'm sorry I suggested you were not what you portrayed yourself to be. In part, I was influenced by a memory which coloured my judgment."

It was like pressing the trigger on a shotgun loaded with bitter pellets. "A *memory!*" she fired at him, her eyes meeting his in a raging blaze of feeling. "You didn't even stop to ask why I was there in New Orleans, doing what I was doing. You know nothing about me except..." Her teeth were bared in savage scorn. "...you happened to see me one night, leading a haunted history tour.''

He winced.

She kept on blasting. ''And for that you decide I'm little better than a whore, pulling tricks, fleecing people, using whatever sex appeal I have to get out of trouble…''

''I didn't say that,'' he whipped back, frowning at the vehemence of her attack.

''You *thought* it. And you had no right to think it, no reason to think it. It was you…you…who took liberties with me. Touching and…and suggesting…'' A tide of heat was rushing up her neck, flooding into her cheeks, making her wish she hadn't brought up any reminder of how he had mused over how well they might go in bed together.

He took a deep breath and calmly said, ''I'm sorry if any action of mine made you feel uncomfortable.''

''*If…if?*'' His calmness incensed her. ''You set out to do it. You know you did,'' she wildly accused. ''Even in your office. Why didn't you just hand me back my hat instead of…''

''It wasn't deliberate. It was pure impulse.''

''I didn't invite it.''

''No, you didn't.'' His mouth curved ironically. ''Except by being an exceptionally attractive woman.''

She shook her head not accepting this excuse. ''It showed a lack of proper respect for me.''

''Oh, come on, Nicole!'' he chided, impatience with her argument slipping through the reins of his control.

He started walking towards her, gesturing a mocking dismissal of her case against him. "You can hardly call putting your hat on your head and touching your cheek major violations. You didn't protest. Didn't flinch away. In fact…"

"Well, please take note of my evasive action right now, Matt King," she flung at him, marching pointedly to the other side of the billiard table to put it between them. "I don't want you near me," she stated bitingly.

"Fine!" he snapped, having already halted. Black derision glittered from his eyes. "I'd have to give you full marks for the drama queen performance."

"So much for your apology!" she mocked.

"A pity you weren't gracious enough to accept it," he shot back at her.

Her chin tilted in defiant challenge. "What's it worth when you're still casting me in a false light and not admitting to any fault yourself?"

"I might have cast you in a false light, lady, but you helped me do it, floundering around as you did in the park."

"And before that? Your *memory* from New Orleans?"

"Yes," he admitted.

From no more than a superficial look at her.

While her memories…the sadness of them still gutted her…although she was glad she had them.

"And just what were you doing there ten years ago?" she asked, still fiercely resenting his interpretation of one brief view of her.

"Seeing some of the world before settling down to family business," he answered with a dismissive shrug.

A wild youthful spree. Totally carefree.

The contrast between them could not have been wider. Emotion welled as she remembered the heavy weight of her responsibility that year. Impossible to keep it out of her voice. She looked directly at Matt King, wanting to nail home how very mistaken he was about her, but even he faded from her mind as she spoke, the memories sharpening, taking over.

"Well, I was *on* family business. My father was dying of cancer and his last wish was to go back to New Orleans. He was a jazz musician and to him it was his soul city. We had very little money but I took him there and got what work I could to help support us. Every night he sat in Preservation Hall, right across the street from Reverend Zombie's Voodoo Shop, where the haunted history tours started and ended. In case you don't know, Preservation Hall is revered by jazz musicians all around the world. It's where…"

"I know," he broke in. "I dropped in there one evening."

She stared at him, wondering if he'd seen or met her father, heard him perform. A lump rose in her throat. She had to swallow hard to make her voice work and even then it came out huskily.

"Some nights when my father wasn't too ill, he'd be invited to play the drums. He was a great jazz drummer."

"*Ollie's Drum*," he murmured.

"You know? You heard him play?"

He shook his head. "I only know about the book you wrote."

"The book…" Tears blurred her eyes. "He was a genius on the drums. Everybody said so. A legend. There were so many stories…"

"Did he die over there?"

She nodded, trying to blink back the tears, but she could see the jazz bands playing in the streets behind the coffin and the tears kept gathering, building up.

"I'm sorry, Nicole. I really am sorry."

She nodded. The quiet voice sounded sincere. Though somehow it wasn't important anymore.

"Please…go," she choked out, not wanting to cry in front of him.

He hesitated a moment then gruffly said, "Believe me. You do have my respect."

Without pressing anything else he left the room, closing the door quickly to give her the privacy she needed. Her chest was so tight it felt like a dam about to burst. She felt her way around the billiard table, reached the chair in front of her desk and sagged onto it. She didn't see the plastic bag with the Kauri Pine Park logo this time. She wasn't seeing anything.

It was ten years since she had buried her father.

It felt like yesterday.

And the loneliness of not having anyone to love, or anyone to love her, was overwhelming.

CHAPTER NINE

ONCE Matteo had headed off to the billiard room, Isabella Valeri King moved from the loggia to the library. She sat at her desk, her work diary in front of her, giving some semblance of purpose. She'd opened it to the one date she wanted to discuss with Matteo when he came to say goodbye to her, but work was not on her mind.

There was trouble between Matteo and Nicole—a sure sign they had connected on a personal level, but not a good result so far.

Nicole stiffened up every time his name was mentioned. Even more so since her visit to the park. And there had been no need for her to work today. Even her argument that Sundays were best for chatting to the old Italian families held no weight since the current members of the family she was writing about had all been gathered here—an easy opportunity to get their input on any facet of the history.

Nicole's choice—her very determined choice against the much-pressed invitation to stay and join them for the luncheon—spelled out a resolution to avoid Matteo at all costs. Quite clearly he had been just as resolved on forcing a meeting, staying on at the castle as long as he had and acting like a cat on hot bricks when Rosita had informed them of Nicole's return.

Such strong resolution had to have passion behind it, Isabella decided. Indifference did not give rise to such behaviour. The trick was to channel the passion into a positive direction. She hoped whatever was going on in the billiard room right now was getting rid of the negatives.

Pride could play the very devil in trying to get two people together. Isabella suspected that pride was a big factor here. It was a pity she didn't know what had caused a conflict to erupt between them, but neither of them would welcome interference on her part, anyway. Though, of course, she could stage-manage opportunities for them to reach out to each other…if they wanted to.

Desire…

It had to be there.

Matteo had clearly been distracted today, not his usual cheerful self at all. Brooding over Nicole's absence, Isabella had concluded. Not even celebrating Hannah's pregnancy had kept his spirits lifted for long. The jokey chatting with his brothers had seemed forced, and his conversation with her after everyone else had gone, had been peppered with silences. But he'd come very briskly to life at Rosita's further announcement that Nicole had gone to the billiard room to work.

"I'll just check that Ms. Redman has everything she needs from me before I leave," he'd said.

Which could have been done by telephone anytime.

The desire for physical confrontation had been paramount.

Desire…passion…surely it was the right mix.

Isabella was clinging to this hope when Matteo appeared in the doorway to the library. Her mind instantly dictated acute observation.

"I'm off, Nonna. Great luncheon. Happy news about the baby. You must be pleased."

Short staccato sentences, his mouth stretched into a smile but not a twinkle of it in his eyes, tension emanating from him as he quickly crossed the room to drop a goodbye kiss on her cheek.

"Yes, I am. Pleased for Antonio and Hannah, too. It's what they wanted," she replied, wishing Matteo would confide what *he* wanted.

He hadn't won whatever he'd gone to win from Nicole Redman. His kiss had no feeling in it, a quick performance of what was expected of him before he left. His mind was clearly preoccupied, and not with happy thoughts. Isabella spoke quickly to hold him with her long enough to ascertain his mood towards Nicole.

"I was just looking through my diary."

"Mmm…" No interest. Mental and physical withdrawal under way.

"I trust you have marked Gina's premiere night on your calendar."

He halted beside her desk, frowning at the reminder of his sister-in-law's debut on the stage of the Galaxy Theatre in Brisbane. "When is it again?"

"Two weeks from this coming Thursday. I've booked six seats on a flight to Brisbane that afternoon."

"Six? Won't Alex and Gina be down there already?"

"Naturally. In fact, Alex will have the children there, too, during the last week of rehearsals. He doesn't want Gina worrying about them when she has to concentrate on her singing. Such a big role, playing Maria in *West Side Story*.''

''She's got the voice for it,'' Matteo said dismissively. He gave her a hooded look. ''So who are the six seats for? Tony, Hannah, you, me...''

''Rosita and Nicole.''

A pause. Then in a voice stripped of any telltale expression he asked, ''Nicole will be going?''

Not *Ms. Redman* this time, Isabella noted. ''Yes. She's very keen to hear Gina sing. And see Peter Owen's production of the show. Such a charming man, Peter. He flew up last weekend to iron out some production details with Gina and dropped in to visit me. Gave Nicole a personal invitation to the post-premiere party he's throwing and she was very happy to accept.''

Matteo's jaw tightened.

Peter Owen had a very *colourful* reputation as a latter-day Casanova. Alex had once been quite jealous of his professional association with Gina. It had spurred him to declare his love for her very publicly. Isabella reflected that a highly competitive streak ran through each of her grandsons' characters. Perhaps the threat of Peter Owen's winning charm would sort out Matteo's feelings towards Nicole.

''I've also booked hotel accommodation for all of us that night,'' she went on. ''Does that suit you or do you want to make alternative plans?''

His brow was lowered broodingly. His silence went on so long, Isabella was drawn into a terse command. ''You can't miss the premiere, Matteo. If only to support Gina, you must go.''

His hand sliced the air. "No question, Nonna. Alex would kill me if I didn't turn up."

"Well, what is the problem? You seem...very distracted."

He grimaced. "Sorry. I'll go along with the arrangements you've made. I suppose it will be red carpet at the theatre. Limousines. Formal dress."

"You can count on it. Peter Owen wouldn't have it any other way."

"The ultimate showman. Well, we'll see, won't we?" he muttered darkly and headed for the door, holding up a hand in a last salute. "'Bye, Nonna. Fax a schedule to my company office and I'll toe the line like a good little boy."

He flashed a mocking smile and was gone.

Definitely not a happy man, Isabella thought.

However, she had achieved the setting for the next scene between Matteo and Nicole, and put in a clever little needle by throwing Peter Owen into the ring. Control of the seating in the plane and in the theatre was hers. As long as neither of the antagonists found some rock-solid excuse for not following through on their given word, they'd have to bear each other's company for many hours.

Isabella smiled to herself.

There was nothing like enforced time together to wear down barriers.

CHAPTER TEN

MATT arrived at Cairns Airport twenty minutes before their flight to Brisbane was scheduled to take off. He didn't have to check any luggage through. A suit bag encased the formal clothes he had to wear to the premiere tonight and a small carry-on bag held the rest of his needs.

Tony met him in the entrance hall, handing over his ticket and seat allocation. "The others have gone through to the departure lounge. Ready to join them?"

"Sure! I guess I'll be sitting next to Nicole Redman on the flight," he commented casually, trying to feel relaxed about it as they strolled towards the security barrier.

"No. Nicole took off early this morning. Nonna said she wanted to spend the day in Brisbane, going through newspaper archives."

Anger blazed through him. She was using the excuse of work to avoid him again. Okay the first time. He had cast slurs on her integrity. But he'd gone out of his way to admit he was wrong and apologise for the offence given. It was definitely not okay a second time. This was a deliberate snub.

"What does she hope to find there?" he asked, barely

keeping his anger in check. Some show of interest was called for since he'd brought up her name.

"Well, you know Nonna's husband and brother were on the same boat that sailed from Brisbane when they went off to the Second World War. Nicole wanted some background stuff on how it was for them."

Naturally it *sounded* reasonable, using the plane ticket to serve two purposes. Very conscientious, too, saving Nonna the expense of funding an extra research trip to Brisbane. Except saving dollars was not what this family history project was about and Nonna would not have blinked an eye at any expense it incurred anywhere along the line. So there was no doubt in Matt's mind that Nicole Redman had deliberately engineered this arrangement to thumb her nose at him and his apology.

"Tough luck, Matt! You'll have to put up with your own company for the next two hours," Tony tossed at him teasingly.

"No problem." He laid his bags on the roller table and they stepped through the security gate without setting off any bells.

"Got to hand it to Nicole," Tony rambled on. "Not leaving a stone unturned to do a thorough job on our family history."

"Seems that way," Matt answered non-committally, collecting his bags and glancing around the departure lounge to spot where the others were seated.

"Over there…" Tony pointed, then grinned at him. "You must be losing your touch, Matt. Gorgeous girl more interested in her work than getting acquainted with you.''

He shrugged. ''I'm probably not her type.''

''Can I take it that's mutual? She's not your type?''

Matt rolled his eyes at him. ''Give it a rest, Tony. I know you're a happily married man but I don't need any matches made for me.''

Certainly not with a fiery little number who wasn't reasonable enough to let her rage go. No, she had to keep rubbing in how offensive he'd been, despite his complete backdown and apology. And to think he'd actually bought the book about her father's life and read it to see where she was coming from, just so he could make his peace with her on this trip, even lying awake half of last night, working out what to say...all for nothing!

He greeted his grandmother, Rosita and Hannah just as the boarding call for their flight was announced. No need to make conversation, which suited him very well because he wasn't in the mood for social chitchat. On the plane he had a window seat with no one next to him. The stewardess handed him a newspaper and he used it to close out everyone else.

His eyes skimmed the print but nothing sank into his consciousness. The empty seat beside him was a constant taunting reminder of Nicole Redman's deliberate absence from it. No truce from her. She'd probably arrange for her seat in the theatre tonight to be the furthest from him. And no doubt she'd ride in the limousine transporting his grandmother and Rosita and he'd be directed to ride with Hannah and Tony and Alex.

Which was fine by him.

He didn't care what she did.

She could flirt her head off with Peter Owen at the post-premiere party, too, and he wouldn't turn a hair. In fact, he'd feel utter contempt for it because it would be an act of blatant dishonesty, pretending she fancied Peter Owen. He hadn't been wrong about the sexual attraction she'd felt with him. She could deny it as much as she liked. He knew better.

She would have let him kiss her out on the veranda, after he'd removed the butterflies from her hair. She had not recoiled from his touch one bit. What did she expect a man to do, anyway? Hold back until she gave verbal permission to come close? Ignore the body language that was telling him he was welcome and wanted?

Just let her try that fruit-tasting exercise with Peter Owen and Casanova Pete would be dragging her under the table to take what she was offering. Given the desire she had aroused, Matt figured he'd been a positive gentleman. And what had he got for his restraint? Lies and abuse.

His fault that she hadn't been able to concentrate on the job!

What absolute rot!

She'd had sex on her mind, same as he had, and he hadn't made one suggestive remark to feed her fantasies all the time they'd been walking through the park. It was totally perverse to blame her thoughts on him. She'd made them up all by herself. So why the hell couldn't she admit it instead of scuttling behind a defence of *his fault?*

She might not like wanting him.

He didn't like wanting her.

That didn't change the truth.

Matt seethed over this truth all the way to Brisbane. He was still seething over it when they booked into the hotel, more so when he reached his room and tossed his things on the queen-size bed, which reminded him how open he'd been in laying out what he'd felt to Nicole Redman, stating an obvious desire when wondering out loud how they might be together in bed.

He'd been wrong about her ability to do the job, wrong about her trading on her looks and being unfair to his grandmother, but even with all his wrong assumptions, he'd offered to smooth the situation over by getting whatever extra help she needed. But did she appreciate he'd been bending over backwards to keep her in Port Douglas? To get rid of the deceit and set up a platform of trust so they could move forward into a relationship that he wouldn't feel bad about?

No!

She couldn't even admit he was right about the mutual lust.

He snatched up the bedside telephone, pressed the button for reception and asked for her room number. He glanced at his watch as the information was given to him. Five-thirty. Everyone in their party was to meet in the hotel lobby at seven-fifteen, ready to be transported to the theatre, and be damned if he was going to be snubbed by Nicole Redman again!

He'd sort this out right now.

She had to be in her room. Women always took forever getting ready for a big night out and tonight was *big* for the family. She'd be aware of when his grandmother was arriving at the hotel, aware that she should be on hand to assure her employer that time was not a problem. Work would definitely be over for today. No one of any sensibility would mess with tonight.

No point in trying to talk to her over the telephone. No way would he give her the satisfaction of hanging up on him. This had to be face to face. And there wasn't one bit of guilt she could throw at him this time. With a burning sense of righteousness, Matt left his room and strode towards Nicole Redman's.

Nicole was luxuriating in a bubble bath. Some sensual pampering was precisely what she needed to relax the tension that had made her feel edgy all day. It was impossible to completely avoid Matt King tonight. She simply had to accept that and keep as much distance between them as she could.

Though she still couldn't stop her mind from circling around him, especially knowing she would be seeing him soon. No doubt he would look even more handsome in formal dress. Every man did. It wasn't fair that *he* was so *physically* attractive. It made her feel she might be missing out on some extra-special experience with such a powerhouse of masculinity.

And she wasn't sure she liked the entirely feline instinct that had drawn her into buying a dress she didn't
really need. She'd brought one with her that would do
for tonight. This afternoon's wild rush of blood to the
head had resulted in sheer unnecessary extravagance.
She shouldn't have gone into the shopping mall that
housed such an alluring range of designer boutiques,
courting temptation. The moment she'd seen the black
dress, her mind was consumed by one burning thought...

I'll show him.

Show him what? That she could look attractive, too?
Or were her claws out, wanting to get under his skin as
much as he got under hers. From afar, of course, so he'd
sizzle with frustration...if he still fancied a session in
bed with her. Justice, she'd told herself, turning the in-
sults he'd handed out into savage regret on his part.
After all, he'd savaged her with his outrageously false
reading of her character.

Though he had apologised.

Far too late.

Such a late apology couldn't begin to make up for
how he'd made her feel for over a week of miserable
days and even more miserable nights.

All the same, maybe she shouldn't wear the dress.
Maybe she should return it to the boutique and get her
money back. Being vengeful wasn't about to result in
anything good. It just kept her thinking about him and
his response to her.

Was that a knock on her door?

Yes.

Nicole hauled herself out of the bubble bath, thinking it might be Hannah dropping by for a little chat before they had to dress, probably unable to contain her excitement over Gina's premiere, wanting to share it. She had raved to Nicole about Gina's voice, certain that her sister-in-law was going to be a star in tonight's show, but first-night nerves might have got to her.

Nicole gave herself a quick towelling, then wrapped herself in the big white bathrobe supplied by the hotel as she hurried through the bedroom. Another knock urged her into faster action. Without pausing to check the identity of the caller, she opened the door and stood in paralysed shock at being confronted by Matt King.

With him standing right in front of her, barely an arm's length away, she was swamped by how big he was, how male he was, and all of him bristling with aggression, sending an electric charge through every nerve of her body. She was instantly and acutely conscious of her nakedness under the bathrobe, and the blistering force of his glittering dark gaze reminded her that her hair was piled carelessly on top of her head, pinned there to keep it out of the bathwater.

"Let's talk, shall we?" he said in belligerent challenge, stepping forward, driving her back from the door and the intimidating power of his advancing presence.

She was hopelessly unprepared for this. It didn't even occur to her to try and stop him as he entered her room and closed the door behind him. She was too busy back-pedalling to put some distance between them, checking that the tie-belt was tied, clutching the lapels of the robe together to prevent any gap from opening, catching her breath enough to speak.

"What do you want to talk about?"

He looked at her mouth. Was it quivering? She had no make-up on, no armour at all in place to give her any confidence in maintaining some personal dignity against the raw onslaught of his sexuality.

His gaze dropped to the hollow in her throat. She could feel the dampness there that she hadn't had time to wipe away. He took in the clutching position of her hands on the hotel robe, an obvious pointer to how vulnerable she felt. His eyes missed nothing. He probably saw her toes curling as he looked at her bare feet, and he surely absorbed every curve of her body as his gaze slowly travelled back up to her face, her mussed hair, her eyes.

"Maybe talking isn't what either of us want," he said gruffly, his deep voice furred with the desire for a more primitive means of man/woman communication.

Sheer panic galloped through her heart, contracted her stomach, shot tremulous waves down her thighs. "I don't know what you mean," she gabbled, her mind totally seized up with a clash of fear and excitement.

"Yes, you do." His eyes mocked her denial as he moved forward and cupped her chin, fingers lightly fanning the line of her cheek. "You know exactly what I mean, Nicole Redman. The only question is...will you give an honest response?"

He was going to kiss her.

And she just stood there, mesmerised by the blazing

purpose in his eyes, mesmerised by the tingling warmth of the feather-light caress on her cheek, allowing his cupping thumb to tilt her chin to a higher angle, a readily kissable angle, and when his mouth covered hers, it wasn't just her lips yearning to know what his kiss would be like. Her whole body was zinging with anticipation, vibrantly alive to whatever sensations this man would impart.

It wasn't a gentle kiss. She hadn't expected it to be. Didn't want it to be. He'd churned her up so much, the need for some outlet for all the pent-up feelings crashed through her, urging answers from him. His mouth was hotly demanding and hers demanded right back, no holds barred as they merged in a rage of passion that craved satisfaction.

An arm clamped around her back, slamming her against him. The hand that had been holding her face to his, raked through her hair, dislodging pins, exulting in freeing the long tresses, and she exulted in it, too. She revelled in being pinned to the hard surging strength of his powerful physique, loved the feel of his hand in her hair, its aggressive need to tangle in the long soft silkiness of it.

Somehow it freed her to touch him as she liked; the muscular breadth of his shoulders, the wiry curls at the back of his neck. Every contact with him was intensely exciting, the squash of her breasts against the firm hot wall of his chest, the pulsating sense of their hearts drumming to the same fierce escalation of desire for each other, thighs rubbing, pressing, wanting flesh against flesh.

She felt the tie-belt on the robe being yanked, pulled apart. Matt wrenched his mouth from hers, dragging in air as he lifted his head back. His eyes glittered an intense challenge as he moved his hands to hook under the collar of the robe, intent on sliding it from her shoulders. He didn't speak. He didn't have to. The words zapped straight into her mind.

Stop me now if you want to stop.

Her mouth throbbed with the passion he'd fired. Her breasts ached to be touched, kissed, taken by him. Her whole body was aroused, screaming for the ultimate intimacy with this man, uncaring of any moment beyond the experience he was holding out to her.

She didn't speak.

As her hands slid down from his shoulders to make the disrobing easy, her eyes told him there'd be no stopping from her and it wasn't a surrender to his will. It was her choice. And it was up to him to prove the choice was worth taking.

He eased back from her to let the robe slither to the floor. He didn't look down at the nakedness revealed. His gaze remained fastened on hers, the challenge still very much in force as he brought her hands up to his chest, resting them beside the buttons on his shirt.

"Don't give me passive," he growled. "Show me. Get rid of my shirt."

He released her hands. He stood there, inviting her touch but not forcing it. She could feel the burning pride behind his stance, the tension of not knowing whether she might refuse, the determination not to leave himself open to any accusation that he'd taken unfair advantage of her, yet the wanting was not in any way diminished. The heat of it was sizzling around her, bringing tingles to her bare skin and the sense of partnership he was demanding acted like a heady intoxicant to the cocktail of excitement already stirred.

Her hands moved with eager purpose. He'd stripped her naked. He had to be naked, too. She wanted him to be, wanted to feast her eyes on all that made him so masculine, wanted to touch, to absorb the power of him, to experience exactly what it was that compelled such a strong sexual response in her, even against her will, against her reason. She didn't want to fight it now. She had to know.

The shirt was open. She slid it from his shoulders. Warm, satin-smooth skin, tightly stretched over firm muscles. His chest was magnificent. She couldn't resist grazing her fingers through the little nest of black curls below his throat, gliding her palms down towards his flat stomach.

It spurred him out of his tense immobility. It was *his* hands that unfastened his trousers, got rid of the rest of his clothes, stripping with a speed that was breath-taking in its effect of instantly revealing more than she had let herself imagine. He was a big man, big all over, and a little shiver ran through her at the thought of mating with him.

Too late to back off now.

Besides, she didn't want to.

Her heart was thundering in her ears. Her whole body was at fever-pitch anticipation. And there was a wanton primitive streak inside her that was wildly elated when his strong hands gripped her waist, lifted her off her feet and swung her onto the bed.

He loomed over her, all dominant male, and there was a fierce elation in his eyes at having won what he wanted. Though she knew it wasn't true. She was the one taking him. And her eyes beamed that straight back at him. No surrender. A searing challenge to complete what had been started, complete it to *her* satisfaction.

It was like a battle of minds…a battle of hearts… intensely exhilarating…all-consuming…concentration totally focused. There was no foreplay…none needed… none wanted…just this apocalyptic coming together… the ultimate revelation of all the uncontrollable feelings they had struck in each other.

Every nerve in her body seemed to be clustered in that one intimate place, highly sensitised, waiting, poised to react to his entry. There was a tantalisingly gentle probing, a teasing test of how welcome he was. Instinctively, needfully, she clasped him with her legs, urging him on. He plunged forward and her whole body arched up in ecstatic pleasure at the sense of him filling her with his power. It was glorious, having him so deeply inside her, then feeling him thrust there over and over again. Her own muscles joyously adjusted to his rhythm, revelling in the exquisite sensations, craving more and more peaks of pleasure.

Her whole being was centred on how it was with him. She'd never felt anything like it in her entire life, hadn't known what was possible. She lost all sense of self. This was fusion on such an intense level there was no room for any other reality and even when she reached the first incredibly sweet climax, it simply set her afloat on a sea of pleasure that kept on rolling with waves that crested even more deliciously.

How he held his climax back for so long she didn't know, but when it came it was wondrous, too, the fast friction, the powerful surge of energy, the explosion of heat spilling deeply inside her...and a feeling of over-whelming love burst through her, tingling right to her scalp, her fingertips, her toes. And she found herself hugging him to her, hugging him with every ounce of strength she had left in her arms and legs.

His arms burrowed under her and hugged her right back, and there was no letting go, even when he rolled onto his side. He carried her with him, as blindly and compulsively intent as she was on holding on to the togetherness. Time had no meaning. Nothing had any meaning but this.

Until the telephone rang.

CHAPTER ELEVEN

THE telephone!

The realisation of where she was and what she was supposed to be doing came like a thunderclap, jerking Nicole up from Matt King's embrace. Eyes wide open with the shock of having lost track of everything, her gaze instantly targeted the radio clock on the bedside table: 18:33. Only forty minutes left to get ready for tonight's premiere and be down in the lobby for the trip to the theatre!

"Look at the time! We've got to move!" she shot at Matt, heaving herself off him and rolling to the side of the bed to pick up the receiver.

"Right!"

The quick agreement helped to get her mind focused on dealing with the situation. First the call, which was probably from her employer to ask about today's research—her employer who was footing the bill for this hotel accommodation which had just been used for…nothing at all to do with the agenda Isabella Valeri King had approved for today and tonight!

It was some relief to feel Matt moving off the other side of the bed, going straight into action. Nicole swung her legs onto the floor, sat up straight, took a deep breath, lifted the receiver to her ear, and spoke in a reasonably even tone.

The caller *was* Mrs. King.

Nicole quickly expressed satisfaction in the information she'd collected from newspaper archives, replied to various other queries about her day, gave assurances that her hotel room was fine and she hadn't forgotten the seven-fifteen deadline in the lobby, lied about having had something to eat, and every second that ticked by increased the tension of losing more time.

She had her back turned to Matt but she could hear him moving around, pulling on clothes. No sound of his exit, though. Which doubled her tension as she managed to conclude the call. Bad enough that she'd had no option but to remain naked while he dressed. What was he waiting for? Didn't he understand there was no acceptable excuse for not being punctual tonight? And it would be dreadfully inappropriate not to be properly dressed and groomed, as well.

Her heart pitter-pattered nervously. What was his reaction now to what had transpired between them? Had it been as world-shaking for him as it had been for her? Suddenly feeling intensely vulnerable, she forced herself to look at him over her shoulder, needing some reassurance that he had been deeply affected, too.

He stood near the short passageway to the door, his gaze trained very intently on her. He was fully dressed, looking every bit as respectable as when he'd entered, ready to meet anything or anyone.

''Don't try skipping out on me tonight, Nicole,'' he

fired at her, his eyes blazing a command that promised she would rue any deviation from what was planned. ''You *be* in the hotel lobby at seven-fifteen. We'll take it from there.''

He was gone before Nicole could even catch her breath. He'd brought an electrifying wave of aggression into her room and his exit left her with the same sense of force which would not be denied, no matter what ensued from this moment.

It stunned her into losing a few more moments.

Her mind rallied to examine what he'd said since it had to be a lead to what he was feeling. *Skipping out on him...* Was that how he viewed her choice to take an earlier flight today? Perhaps even further back, a reference to the family luncheon she'd deliberately missed.

He must have taken both absences as very personal slights. Which they were. But this had to mean he'd been thinking about her as much as she'd been thinking about him, and getting highly riled about it. And he wasn't about to walk away from what had just happened.

Be there!

The command of a very determined man to have her with him. He certainly hadn't had enough of her. Which was fine by Nicole. She hadn't had enough of him, either. Which brought a crooked little smile to her face. She'd leapt in at the deep end with Matt King and didn't know if she'd be able to keep her head above these turbulent waters. But she wasn't about to drown yet.

The black taffeta dress.

Yes, she'd be there in the lobby at seven-fifteen, but

not as a woman submissive to his will. In fact, she'd do her absolute utmost to knock his eyes out. Teach him not to take anything about her for granted.

Matt was the first down. He was early. Eight minutes past seven. He hoped to catch his grandmother before Nicole appeared and ensure the *right* seating in the limousines and at the theatre. He didn't care if this raised her eyebrows or gave her satisfaction. Nicole Redman had certainly proved his match in bed but that didn't mean marriage was on the line.

Ten past seven. Matt breathed a sigh of relief as he saw Rosita, Alex and his grandmother emerge from an elevator. Alex, as always, looked impressive and totally in control of himself. Nonna was in royal-blue silk, very regal with her head of white hair held high and all her best jewellery on. Rosita wore burgundy lace and was beaming with excitement. They all smiled at him.

Matt forced a smile he didn't feel, knowing he should be sharing their anticipation of pleasure in the show and a triumphant night for Gina. All he could think of was getting Nicole Redman to himself again. As the others joined him in the middle of the lobby, he directly addressed his grandmother.

''So what's the arrangement, Nonna? You three go in the first limousine, the rest of us to follow?''

She appeared to consider, then slowly answered, ''Nicole may want to ride with us.''

''Won't look good for the red carpet arrival at the theatre,'' he argued. ''I think Alex should take both your arm and Rosita's for the walk in. Which would make Nicole the odd woman out. Better that she be accompanied by me, stepping out of the second limousine.''

''Matt has a point there, Nonna,'' Alex remarked supportively. ''Peter has lined up media coverage. Bound to be cameras on us.''

Was that a smug little smile flitting across her lips? Certainly there was a twinkle in her eyes as she answered, ''Then we will do it Matteo's way.''

Inwardly he bridled against seeming to fall into her matchmaking trap. He didn't pursue the issue of seating at the theatre, deciding he'd hold on to Nicole's arm so that any separation would not occur, unless she made a point of it. Unlikely that she would carry out a public snub in these circumstances.

The problem was Matt didn't feel sure of her, despite the intimacy they had just shared. Giving in to mutual lust behind closed doors didn't guarantee a positive response in other areas. They hadn't talked, hadn't reached any kind of understanding he could feel comfortable with.

Maybe she'd just been satisfying a sexual curiosity, an itch that needed scratching, and she'd back right off him again now. He found his hands clenching and forced himself to relax. She had to stay beside him for the next few hours. At least that much was assured.

Tony and Hannah emerged from another elevator, Hannah looking absolutely fantastic in a beaded green gown, her long crinkly blond hair billowing around her shoulders. Pregnancy not showing yet.

Matt checked the time on his watch again. Thirteen minutes past seven. If Nicole wasn't here in the next two minutes he'd go up to her room and haul her down. No way was he going to let her call in sick or make some other lame excuse for not joining him tonight. If she thought she could take him for sexual pleasure, then turn her back on him... Matt seethed over the possibility, vowing he'd set her straight in no uncertain terms.

He caught his grandmother observing him and tried to adopt a nonchalant air, glancing around the lobby in a pretence of careless patience for their party to be complete. An image of red and black caught his eye, high in his normal field of vision. His gaze jerked up. There, at the top of the staircase, leading down to the lobby from the mezzanine floor.

She stood looking straight at him.

Checking him out?

Matt neither knew nor cared. His heart turned over as he slipped back in time to the night he'd first seen her in New Orleans. Red and black. And her skin glowing pearly white. Stunning. Fascinating. Compelling him to follow, to watch her, listen to her. Not the time nor place to get to know her then, but now...

"Oh, there's Nicole on the mezzanine level," he heard his grandmother say. "She must have pressed the wrong button in the elevator."

No, Matt thought. It was deliberate.

Her gaze didn't so much as waver from his as she began her descent to the lobby. He wasn't someone in a mask at the back of a crowd of tourists tonight. She knew who he was and was challenging his interest in her, refiring the desire he'd driven to its ultimate expression earlier, desire she'd conceded herself.

He'd called her a *femme fatale*.

Mockingly.

He could feel her flaunting it in his face with every step she took down the staircase. Her black dress was the sexiest he'd ever seen, its heart-shaped neckline cut wide on the shoulders to little cap sleeves that virtually left her slender white arms bare. The décolletage was low enough to show the valley between her breasts and the upper swell of them on either side. More provocative than blatant. The bodice was moulded to her curves and the whole gown hugged her figure to knee-length. He could see a fishtail train slithering down the steps behind her. The shiny fabric added to the whole sensual effect.

Matt belatedly realised he was moving to meet her. She'd drawn him like a magnet. Too late to stop, to deny her that power. Better to make the action seem perfectly natural, her escort doing the polite thing. He waited at the foot of the stairs, ready to offer his arm, which she'd take if he had to forcibly hook hers around it.

Her hair gleamed like liquid fire, a smooth fall forward over one shoulder, brushed back behind the other. That was provocative, too. Her mouth the same colour red. Her lashes were lowered to make it appear her gaze was focused on the steps, but it wasn't. Through the semi-veil, her eyes were simmering with satisfaction at having him waiting on her.

Matt had to quell a wild surge of caveman instincts.

His family was watching and be damned if he'd give his grandmother the satisfaction of knowing *her choice* was making him burn more than any other woman he'd ever known. Now was the time for very polished manners and Nicole Redman had better match him in that.

He offered his arm as she took the last step, his own eyes hooded to prevent her from seeing the inner conflagration of rampant desire and angry frustration with the situation he found himself in. Control was needed. He hated not having it. He would not let this woman take it from him.

The tightness in his chest eased as she slid her arm smoothly around his, no hesitation at all. "Thank you," she said huskily.

"My pleasure," he replied, darting a sharp look at her, surprised by the furred tone.

Her gaze fluttered away from the quick probe, but he was left with an impression of uncertainty. No triumph. No confidence, either. She wasn't claiming him. In fact, the hand resting on his coat sleeve was actually tremulous. He quickly covered it with his own, holding it in place. If she was having second thoughts about linking herself to him, no way would he allow her to flit off and leave him standing like a fool.

"You look quite superb tonight," he said, determined on appearing outwardly calm and collected as he led her towards the family group.

"So do you," she muttered, then took a deep breath as though she needed it to steady herself.

Was she regretting having had sex with him? Worried

about it? Afraid he might now take some advantage from it she didn't want? Did her appearance have more to do with bravado than deliberate allure?

Alex was ushering his grandmother and Rosita towards the door. Tony and Hannah were hanging back, waiting. Matt waved them on, wanting them to go ahead and give him a few private moments with Nicole.

"We need to do some talking," he shot at her.

Red battle flags in her cheeks. "I thought you'd done all the talking you wanted to do with me."

What was this? Blaming him for what she'd wanted to do herself? "Nowhere near," he mocked. "You could say we now have a basis for a beginning."

"I thought it was an end in itself," came her snippy reply.

"Rubbish! If circumstances were different, we'd still be on that bed."

Her mouth compressed. No reply. She didn't want to admit it and denial would be a lie. He hadn't actually meant sexual communication. Why was she being difficult? Talking had to be the next step. He tried again.

"We don't have the time now but after the show…"

"There's a party and I intend to go to it." She turned her head to direct a blaze of defiance at him. "With you or without you. Please yourself. I will not be dictated to by you, Matt King."

"I had mutual interests in mind," he grated out.

"Above the sexual level?"

It goaded him into retorting, "Something wrong with the sexual level?"

"No. But there's more to me than that."

"You think I don't know it?"

"You haven't shown it."

Her head snapped forward, pride stamped on her tilted profile.

Matt fumed at her intransigence. "Precisely how was I supposed to show it when you've been avoiding me like the plague?"

"You *were* a plague."

"Well, well, progress," he drawled mockingly. "Thank you for the past tense. Satisfying our mutual lust was of some benefit."

Her chin tilted higher, emphasising her long graceful neck. Matt wondered how long it would stay extended if he planted a few hot kisses on it. Going to see *West Side Story* had no appeal to him tonight, even with Gina singing. *The Taming of the Shrew* would have suited him much better.

Ahead of them, Alex was stepping into the first limousine after his grandmother and Rosita. Tony and Hannah were outside the lobby, waiting for the second limousine to slide into place. The hotel doors were being kept open for his and Nicole's imminent passage to the pick-up point.

At least Nicole hadn't queried arrangements. Matt figured he'd won that much from her. And she'd accepted him as her escort. No overt attempt to avoid his physical presence. She might be burning over the fact he hadn't left her with honeyed words after their intimacy, but given the way she'd treated him previously, what could she expect?

He'd been entirely reasonable.

So what the hell was her problem?

"Well, I hope *you* enjoy the show tonight," he said with a twist of irony.

She looked at him, obviously confused by his line of thought. "What do you mean by that?" she asked, her tone wary, suspicious.

"It's about star-crossed lovers, ending unhappily. Which is what you seem determined on for us."

The comment sharpened her eyes into a fine glitter. "You're very fast at assumptions."

"You could try giving me more to work on," he retaliated.

"And you could try asking instead of making up your own scenarios and thinking you can force me into them," she flashed back at him.

"Fine! After the show tonight…"

"I'm going to the party," she said stubbornly.

"So am I," he snapped, having run out of time to say any more.

The first limousine had pulled away, Hannah and Tony were climbing into the second, and he and Nicole were now on their heels, poised to follow. A few seconds later they were all settled inside it and the chauffeur was closing the door on them.

Matt sat facing Tony, almost hating his brother for looking so happy. And there was Hannah next to him, holding his hand, glowing as though all her Christmases had just come. In contrast, he filled the space beside the red-haired witch who kept stirring cauldrons of boiling oil to hang him over them.

But he'd get her tonight.

If she thought she could give him the slip at the post-premiere party, she could think again. He'd be there at every turn, making his presence felt. And she'd feel it all right. He wasn't making any wrong assumptions about the sexual spark between them.

Absolute dynamite.

And the fuse was burning.

CHAPTER TWELVE

THEY had a box at the theatre. Nicole was placed next to Matt in the second row of seats behind Alex and Rosita and Mrs. King, but at least she had Hannah on her other side and the arrangement made for easy conversation amongst the family. She wasn't isolated with Matt, which was an enormous relief since she couldn't trust herself to speak civilly with him.

Not that her inner tension eased much. She was hopelessly aware of him. Their physical intimacy had heightened it a hundredfold, making her acutely conscious of her sexuality and his. It played on her mind so much she could barely think of anything else. Back in the hotel lobby, she'd ended up snapping at him out of her own resentment that it could be so overwhelming.

Other things should be more important. Respect, love, trust, understanding…what about them? And he was so arrogant, confident of claiming her whenever he wanted, and the worst part was she was quivering inside, yearning for what he'd given her to be given again. How was she going to handle this? How? What was the best way? Was there a best way?

Star-crossed lovers…ending unhappily.

Those insidious words lingered in her mind as the show started but she was soon caught up in the Romeo and Juliet story being played out on the stage. The production was vibrant and intensely emotional with its continual overtone of tragedy looming, the inevitable outcome of irreversible conflict.

Every time Gina sang there was an almost breathless silence throughout the theatre, the poignant power of her voice and the empathy she drew from the audience made her a wonderful Maria. The rest of the cast put in very good performances but she shone, and at interval the buzz of excitement and pride in the family box put irrepressible smiles on everyone's faces, even Matt's and Nicole's.

The second half of the show was even more heart-wringing. With tears pricking her eyes, Nicole fumbled around her feet for her evening bag, needing tissues. Matt offered a clean white handkerchief. Rather than make any noise, unclicking her bag, she took it, nodding her thanks. It was very handy when Maria's lover was shot and lay dying with Maria kneeling beside him as they sang a last plea of hope for the world to come right—*"Somewhere..."*

Tears gushed.

Nicole mopped frantically, struggling to stop a sob from erupting.

"Hold my hand..." The words were so terribly moving, and when Matt's hand covered hers, squeezing sympathetically, she gripped it and squeezed back as though it were a lifeline to stop her from falling apart.

The curtain came down.

The only sounds in the theatre were sniffles being

smothered and throats being cleared. The applause was slow in coming, a sprinkle of handclaps quickly joined by more, building like a huge wave to a crescendo that urged more and more clapping. Nicole wanted to use her hands but one of them was still entangled with Matt's and she was suddenly acutely conscious of having hung on to it.

His hand.

The warmth and strength of it zinged up her arm. Her heart skipped a beat. She didn't want to let the comforting contact go but was there really any comfort for her in this attraction to Matt King? Embarrassed, she darted him a look of appeal as she wriggled her fingers within his grip. He returned an ironic little smile and released her hand, moving his straight into a long round of applause.

There was an absolute ovation for Gina, many shouts of "Bravo!" She was presented with a huge bouquet of red roses and she smiled directly up at Alex who leaned on the railing of the box and blew a kiss to her. She blew one back to him. Their obvious love for each other gave Nicole a stab of envy.

Why couldn't it... Her head turned to Matt King even before the thought was completed. *...be like that for them?*

He caught her glance and cocked a quizzical eyebrow.

Heat whooshed into her cheeks and she jerked her attention back to the stage. The thought certainly hadn't occurred to him. The expression lingering on his face from having watched the interplay between his brother and sister-in-law was amusement. Did he find real love between a man and a woman a joke? Was sex all he considered?

Or was it all he was considering with *her?*

Nicole found herself pressing her thighs tightly together, a silent, vehement protest against such a limitation, especially when a relationship could be so much more. Surely such strong sexual chemistry had to be linked to some special selective process. It made no sense otherwise.

She was still battling the feelings Matt aroused when Peter Owen, the director of the show, was called on stage to another loud burst of applause. She couldn't help smiling at his air of elated triumph as he took the microphone and made a short speech, thanking the audience for their acclaim, which of course, was richly deserved, and it demonstrated how magnificently perceptive they all were to recognise and acknowledge it.

As always, he was so charmingly over-the-top he drew laughter and more applause, leaving everyone in high spirits as the final curtain came down. *He's still Peter Pan,* Nicole thought fondly, remembering how he'd brought an effervescent lightness to some of her darker hours in the old days, a kindness that felt more like fun than kindness.

Alex stood and spoke to his grandmother. "I'll just slip backstage while the theatre is emptying. I won't be long."

"Take your time, Alessandro. We're in no hurry."

She turned around to smile at Nicole and comment, "Peter made it work wonderfully well, didn't he?"

"A brilliant production," she agreed. "I didn't know he had this in him but he really did pull it off."

The old lady's gaze shifted to Matt. "The ultimate showman," she said with a nod, as though repeating a remark he'd made. Then in a whimsical tone, she added, "Nicole knew Peter when he was just starting out as a pianist, getting the occasional gig with jazz bands."

Matt turned a frown on her. "In the same bands your father played in?"

"Sometimes," she answered evenly, vowing to watch her wayward tongue and invite more normal conversation between them. "He was more a fill-in than a regular. Though I must say I missed him when he dropped out of the Sydney jazz scene. He took a job as a pianist/singer on a cruise ship and sailed out of our lives."

The frown deepened. "You made no mention of him in your book."

He'd read her book?

Her mind scrambled to fit this stunning news into her picture of Matt King. Her heart lifted at the realisation he had to be interested in her as a person to put the time into reading a biography which revealed her background. It couldn't be just sex on his mind!

"You didn't tell me you'd read *Ollie's Drum,* Matteo," his grandmother half queried, one eyebrow arched in surprise.

Nicole stared at him, still processing her own surprise. He sat back, jawline tightening as though he'd just been smacked on the chin. "Since you've contracted Nicole to write our family history, Nonna, it seemed a good idea to see how she'd dealt with her own," he drawled, deliberately eliminating any *personal* interest in the content.

"I trust you were satisfied," Nicole bit out, anger rising at the lengths he'd gone to, checking that she wasn't cheating his grandmother.

"Very much so," he conceded. "The book was very well written and held my interest."

She burned. He'd probably been flipping through it to see if it contained any evidence of her whoring or fleecing people of their money. Her tongue wanted to whip him for thinking so badly of her, but she restrained it, remembering her outburst in the billiard room when he had apologised for misjudging her.

He had apologised.

He'd even said he respected her.

But then he'd bedded her with only the barest pause for her consent. Nothing to make her feel appreciated or valued. Just straight into sex, since her book had proved she was okay and there probably wouldn't be any nasty comebacks. She hated him for it, hated herself for having been a willing party to it, but in this company she had to appear civil.

"Thank you," she aimed at him, then forced a smile at his grandmother. "To get back to the show, I do think the staging was excellent, but Peter obviously knew what he had in Gina and she certainly delivered it for him."

"Oh, yes!" came the ready agreement. "From the

time he first heard her sing, he was determined on show-casing her talent.''

''Well, he sure did it tonight,'' Hannah chimed in, giving Nicole the opening to turn to her and chat on until Alex returned.

This was the signal for them to start making their exit from the box. Alex reported on all the excitement back-stage as they milled out into the corridor. Inevitably Nicole was coupled with Matt again for the walk down the stairs to the foyer of the theatre.

As reluctant as she was to take his arm, common sense argued the stairs could be tricky in her long gown and high heels, and it would be too impolite if she ignored his offer and used the banister instead. Better to suffer his rock-steady support than risk losing her dignity by wobbling or tripping, though she inwardly bridled at having to be close to him, feeling the whole length of his body next to hers.

They trailed after the others and she wished he would quicken his pace to catch up, but if anything he slowed it, frustrating her wish not to be alone with him, not to be reminded of how he had felt naked, how she had felt...

''How old were you when Peter Owen featured in your life?'' he asked, thankfully pouring cold water on her feverish thoughts.

''Ten and eleven,'' she answered, relieved that he wasn't dwelling on the same hot memories.

''Just a kid then,'' he muttered dismissively.

It goaded her into adding, ''I might have been *just a*

kid, but Peter always went out of his way to make me feel welcome in his company."

"Couldn't resist charming even little girls," came the sardonic comment.

"Charm is often in very short supply," she returned tartly. "And I appreciated it very much at the time."

"No doubt you did. Not much charm in waiting around hotels and nightclubs, watching over an alcoholic father and getting him safely home after his gigs."

The soft derision in his voice piqued her into glancing at him. He caught her gaze and his dark eyes were hard and penetrating as he added, "Was he really worth all you gave him of your life, Nicole?"

"You don't understand..."

"No, I don't. He should have been looking after you. What kind of man puts a set of drums and a bottle of whisky ahead of the welfare of a child? You were nine when your mother died. Nine..."

"He was my father," she answered fiercely.

"Yes, and being a father should mean something," he retorted just as fiercely. "Do you imagine that Alex or Tony would ever neglect their responsibility to their children? That they'd let themselves wallow in depression or find oblivion in a bottle, robbing their children of the sense of security they should have?"

"They occupy a different world," she cried defensively.

"They're men."

"All men aren't the same."

"True. But you're a woman now, not a child, and you

should see things how they really were. From the story you've written it's obvious your father could charm birds out of trees when he wasn't completely in his cups. But charm doesn't make up for the rest."

"You're making judgments again about things you don't know," she seethed at him.

His eyes glittered a black challenge back at her. "Well, I do know Peter Owen has been married and divorced twice, and I'm sure his ex-wives were thoroughly charmed by him to begin with. You might keep that in mind at the party."

She sought to explain the difficulties in living with people who were passionately absorbed in creating a unique form of magic. "It's hard…living with musicians. If you don't understand how important it is to them…"

"So important that your needs always have to take a back seat to their kind of self-expression?" He cocked a mocking eyebrow at her. "You've had a long taste of that, Nicole. Was it so sweet?"

It finally dawned on her that he might be jealous of her interest in Peter. Possibly because she'd made such a firm stand about going to the party where she would inevitably meet her old friend again. Now that he knew of their personal connection, was he imagining she wanted to revive it?

She shook her head, dazed at the convoluted way he had used her life with her father to undermine any chance of her being charmed by Peter. The arm holding hers suddenly felt very possessive, as though it wasn't about to let her stray from his side.

They'd reached the foyer and were trailing the rest of the family group out to the street where the limousines were waiting. In a few minutes they'd be on their way back to the hotel where the party was to be held in a private function room. But Matt King wasn't quite finished pressing his point of view.

"You're free now," he went on in a low intense voice. "Free to pursue what *you* want. *Have* what you want. I gave you a choice up in your room, and you chose me. What do you think that says, Nicole? About your needs?"

She didn't know.

She'd been trying to work out what was happening between them and why. It was confusing, disturbing, and she wasn't acting like her normal self at all. There was no time for a reply, which was just as well, because her mind couldn't fasten on one. She followed Tony and Hannah into their limousine and put on a congenial mask for the ride back to the hotel.

Behind it she silently acknowledged Matt King was right about one thing. She was free to pursue whatever she wanted. No personal attachments. Her only responsibilities applied to whatever work she took on, and she no longer accepted a job that didn't appeal to her.

Free…

Was it a deliberate choice not to tie herself to anyone in all these years since her father's death? At first, she'd felt emptied of anything to give to a relationship. Easier to keep associations superficial. Nothing could be demanded of her. The need to become a whole person, by herself, for herself, had probably been more instinctive than thought out, but Nicole now recognised it was what she'd been doing throughout her years at university.

After that, well maybe she'd got into the habit of being alone. But she had felt lonely and there'd been a few men she'd dated for a while. Until the balance of what they'd enjoyed together got heavier and heavier on their side and she simply didn't want to be the one doing the majority of the giving and the understanding to keep the involvement going.

It was like a line drawn in her mind. This much I'll do. No more. But Matt King blurred all the lines, smashing every perception she'd ever had about men. The Kings, she decided, were a different breed. Their family history was telling her so with everything she learnt about them. Strong compelling men. Family men. Men who held what they had, looked after it and built on it.

Was that what she needed?

Was this why Matt King drew such an instinctive response from her, bypassing any rational thought?

She looked down at the hand he'd held.

Did he mean to keep holding it…if she let him?

Or was she a passing fancy?

CHAPTER THIRTEEN

"NICKY!"

Matt gritted his teeth as Peter Owen headed towards them, arms outstretched.

"You look wonderful!"

His bedroom-blue eyes might just get socked out if they kept gobbling her up.

"Who'd have thought that skinny little red-haired kid would bloom into such a beauty?" he raved on, grabbing her upper arms and planting a kiss on both cheeks.

She laughed and bantered, "Who'd have thought Peter Pan would become such a maestro of the theatre?"

Peter Pan was right, Matt thought darkly. The man was forty and still sparkled with the exuberance of a boy who'd never grow up.

"What a premiere! Are you proud of me?" he preened.

Again she laughed. "Immensely. You're Superman tonight."

"That's exactly how I feel. I could leap off tall buildings…"

Pity he didn't do it!

"Well, don't go faster than a speeding bullet," she teasingly advised. "Enjoy the moment."

"Ah…you always were a sweetheart, Nicky dear.

Good to see you! Got to go and mix now but I'll claim a dance from you later.''

Over my dead body!

He shot a grin at Matt. "Look after her. She's very special.''

I don't need you to tell me that.

Matt forced a smile. "Great night, Peter! Well done!''

He paused, lifting a hand in salute to the real star. "Gina sang like the angel she is,'' he said with sincere fervour before moving on to spread himself around.

It made Matt feel mean about his more violent thoughts. He knew there was real affection between Gina and Peter. Even Alex had grown to like the man. Peter was godfather to their baby daughter. But he did have a reputation for being a world-class womaniser.

Matt turned to the woman beside him, taking some encouragement from the fact that she hadn't tried to drift away in the crowd of people at the party. On the other hand, she probably didn't know anyone here, apart from Peter and the King family. Mostly she'd been silent, filling the time by sampling the gourmet finger food being carried around and offered by numerous waiters.

Had his words as they'd left the theatre got through to her?

Her gaze was following Peter's progress through the crowd. Did she want him back in her life? He'd made her laugh. Matt hadn't heard her laugh before. Usually he did share lots of laughter with the women he spent time with. Why was everything so intense with this one?

He was getting obsessed with her, thinking of little

else. Having sex with her hadn't given him any relief from it, either. If anything, it had locked him into a deeper pursuit of the woman she was. He wanted to know how her mind worked, what she felt, how she saw things.

"Do you like being called Nicky?"

She shrugged, not looking directly at him as she flatly answered, "It's a name from a different life."

"One you've moved on from," he pressed, wanting it to be so.

"Yes and no." Her gaze slowly lifted to his, the rich brown of her eyes somehow reflecting a depth of feeling that put him instantly on alert. "Do we ever really leave our past behind? Aren't we the sum of all our years?" A wistful smile flitted across her very kissable lips. "Perhaps even more. Look at you…"

"What about me?"

"You have a heritage to live up to, as well. Don't you feel that?"

"No. I am who I am."

"One of the Kings. Like Alex and Tony whom you invoked earlier as examples of what a father should be. And I'm sure you consider yourself in the same mould. The King mould."

He frowned over this assertion. Pride in his own individuality wanted to deny he was like his brothers, yet they did all have the same background, the same upbringing. There were common factors. And they lived by the same principles, principles that had been hammered into them by their grandmother. Their heritage…

A waiter came by with a tray of drinks, diverting Nicole's attention to it. She picked up a glass of champagne and sipped as though she needed the kick of alcohol. Matt swiped a glass, too, before the waiter moved on. He thought about Nicole's heritage as he sipped.

Her mother had been Irish. She'd met and fallen in love with Ollie Redman when he'd been touring Dublin, married him and came to Australia. There'd been no maternal family in Sydney for Nicole to fall back on when her mother had died. No paternal family, either. Ollie Redman had spent most of his young life in an orphanage. He probably hadn't known what a father should be, having had no role model himself.

People were the sum of their lives...

So what did that make Nicole?

"Why did you take on this project?" he asked, a sixth sense telling him the answer would be enlightening.

She slanted him a half-mocking look. "To find out what a different life was like."

The life of a long-rooted family. That he was part of. Shock stiffened his whole body. Was this why she'd had sex with him? An intimate experience with one of the Kings? The only one who wasn't married?

His mind went into a ferment. She might have been thinking about it ever since they'd met in his office. Certainly when she'd come up to the park, she'd been considering it, wanting it. She'd been eyeing him off as he'd shown her the photographs in his home. If he hadn't put her professionalism on the line, stung her pride...

But they were past that now and tonight she'd taken

what he'd offered without so much as a hesitation. Taken it and revelled in it every bit as much as he had. So she would want more. One taste wasn't enough. It certainly wasn't enough for him. They'd barely begun to explore...*what it was like.*

Her head was slightly bowed as though she was contemplating the contents of her glass. His gaze drifted down the gleaming flame-red fall of her hair, the fine silk of it caressing the bare white skin of her back above the dip of her gown, a dip that revealed the sensual curve of her spine. Below it, her delectable bottom jutted out, begging to be touched. Matt felt himself getting aroused, thighs tightening, sex stirring. He wanted this woman again. Again and again and again.

She was rubbing her index finger idly around the rim of her glass. The urge to snatch it away, force her to look at him and admit what she wanted was strong. Then they could get out of this party, go to his room or hers, and...

"What you said about charm..." She lifted her head and there was sadness in her eyes, making a savage mockery of the desire running rampant through him. "Neither my father nor Peter had family behind them. The charm is a defence against that emptiness, and a reaching out to be liked. A need for everyone to like them, even if it is only on a superficial level."

She paused, her eyes begging some understanding from him. "You don't have that need, Matt. You're very secure in the life you were born into. It makes a difference."

He felt chastened. He *was* more fortunate than others with his family. No denying it. Yet he couldn't imagine himself not making his own way to a life he could be proud of, in every sense. Having to be propped up by others, dependent on what they did for him…no, that was not a situation he'd ever want or accept.

"Maybe it does," he grudgingly conceded. "But in the end, everybody is responsible for what they make of their own lives. There are choices."

And she'd chosen to have sex with him!

She must have read his thought. A tide of heat rushed into her cheeks. He wondered if she cursed her white skin for being such a telltale barometer of her feelings. It gave him a kick, just watching it, though he'd prefer to touch. His hands itched to touch.

"I think choices are shaped by what's gone before," she argued. "People fall into them because…" She stopped, floundering in the face of what she saw in his eyes.

Matt wasn't hiding what he was thinking, what he was wanting. "Because a need pushed them that way?" he finished for her.

"Yes," she whispered.

"And when there's a mutual need, it's even easier to go with it," he pushed, all his energy pumping into drawing her with him. "And why not? Why not see where it leads?"

She stood absolutely still, her gaze fastened on his, her lips slightly parted as though she needed to suck in air, but if she did it was imperceptible. Matt suspected her lungs weren't working at all, seized up with tension, as his were, waiting for the line to be crossed. The fire in her cheeks did not abate. She didn't speak but Matt knew in his bones she wanted what he wanted. An exhilarating recklessness zinged through him.

A waiter approached, offering another tray of fancy canapes. Matt plucked the glass from Nicole's hold, her fingers sliding from it, not clutching. He put both his and her glass on the tray, uncaring that it was carrying food. The action jerked her gaze towards the tray. Matt wasn't about to give her time to regroup. The wave was going his way and ride it he would.

He grabbed her hand, winding his own firmly around it. ''Come with me,'' he commanded and set off, making a path through the partying crowd, pulling her with him.

She didn't try to pull back.

Her acquiescence put a surge of power into his sense of rightness. Nothing was going to stop him. They had to pass by his grandmother and Rosita. He didn't care if they saw or what they thought of him and Nicole leaving together. Let them wonder. It didn't matter.

A phrase from the old *Star Wars* movie clicked into his mind—*The force be with you!* It was with him all right, pounding through his bloodstream, invigorating every muscle in his body, making his skin tingle with electric vitality.

They were finally free of the function room, out in the corridor, heading for the elevators. There was a tug on his hand, a breathless cry, ''Where are you taking me?''

"Where we can be alone together." He paused long enough to release her hand and put his arm around her waist, wanting her clasped close to him, inseparable. He scooped her with him the last few steps to the bank of elevators and pressed the button to give them access to one of them.

"This isn't right," she gasped, still out of breath.

"Oh, yes it is!"

"I think…"

"That's the problem." His eyes blazed his inner certainty at her. "You've been thinking too much since we were interrupted."

Doors slid open.

He swept her into the empty compartment and pressed the button for the floor where his room was situated.

"This is not a grey issue," he stated as the doors slid shut. "It's black and white…" He turned her fully into his embrace, sliding one hand into her glorious hair to hold her head tilted up to his. "…and red," he added with deep satisfaction, loving the feel of her hair and craving the taste of her red mouth.

He kissed her. Her lips felt soft under his, infinitely seductive. Her mouth was far more intoxicating than champagne. It fizzed with passion, exciting all the primitive instincts she stirred in him.

When the elevator doors opened, it triggered the urge to pick her up, keep hold of her. He bent, hooking his arm around her thighs, and sweeping her up against his chest where his heart was beating like a wild tom-tom, drumming him forward.

He was out of the elevator and striding towards his room, his whole being focused on one outcome, when unbelievably, her hand slammed against his shoulder and she began struggling.

"Let me go! Put me down!" Fierce cries, ringing in his ears.

He stopped, looked his puzzlement at her, realised she was in earnest, wanting to be released, so he set her on her feet, still not understanding what the fuss was about.

She wrenched herself out of his hold, whirling to put distance between, then backing towards the elevator, her hands up in a warding-off action, her face blazing with passionate protest.

"I won't let you do this again!"

"Do what?" He was completely perplexed by her reaction. She'd responded to his kiss...

Her breasts heaved as she drew breath to hurl more words at him. "Just taking me when you feel like it."

"Now hold on a minute. You..." He stepped towards her.

"Stop right there!" Her voice cracked out like a whip. "Don't you dare grab me again!"

He stopped, clenching his hands in frustration at this unreasonable outburst. "You came with me, Nicole," he grated out.

"Yes," she snapped. "But I've come to my senses now and I will not come with you any further, Matt King."

"Why not?"

"Because I don't like myself for...for letting your sex

appeal…override everything else. I won't let what happened earlier tonight happen again.''

"It was good. It was great," he argued vehemently.

"That's all you want from me, isn't it? More sexual satisfaction."

"You get it from me, too," he countered hotly knowing full well she'd not gone short on pleasure with him.

Heat scorched her cheeks. "So we're supposed to service each other, are we?"

He could feel his chin jutting out at this crude description, but pride wouldn't let him back down. "Seems like a good idea to me."

She shook her head. "That's not who I am."

"What do you mean?"

"I mean…" Her eyes flashed with scornful pride. "…find someone else to take to your bed. I don't want that kind of relationship."

She turned and jabbed the button to summon an elevator. Matt had the sinking feeling he'd just dug his own grave with her. But how could that be? The wanting *was* mutual. What was wrong with being honest? She'd kissed him back in the elevator. Her body had clung yearningly to his.

"What *do* you want?" he shot at her.

She shook her head. "I'm going back to the party."

Her gaze was fixed on the arrow indicating an elevator rising to this floor.

"Nicole!"

She wouldn't look at him.

"The least you can do is answer me."

"Just…leave me alone…please."

Her voice wobbled. It struck Matt that she was in acute distress, possibly crying. What had he done? Before he could begin to figure out how to fix the situation, an elevator opened and she moved in a frantic flurry, rushing into it and jabbing at the control panel inside the compartment, her head dipped, her hair swishing forward, curtaining her white face. No colour in her cheeks now.

The doors started to slide shut. Matt moved instinctively to block their closure, the urge to fight any closure with Nicole Redman screaming through him.

"Don't! Please, don't! Let me go!" she cried despairingly, flapping her hands at him in wild agitation as she backed up against the rear wall of the small compartment, her eyes swimming with tears, lashes blinking frantically but unable to stop the moist stream from trickling down her cheeks.

"Just tell me what you do want. Whatever it is you think I won't give you," he demanded hoarsely, churned up by her turbulent emotion. "I need an answer."

"*You* need…" Her throat choked up.

She bent her head and wrapped her arms around herself in a protective hug. He could see her swallowing convulsively and wanted to offer comfort, wanted to hold her and soothe her distress away, but her rejection of him made it impossible.

Her head slowly lifted, lifted high, her chin raised in a proud lonely stand, her eyes bleakly haunted by needs that were part of her world, not his.

"I want to be loved," she said in a raw husky voice. "I want someone to care about me. Look after me. My life is empty of that. Empty…"

It was an instantly recognisable truth. No family, no attachments. And from what he'd read in her book, she'd done all the loving and caring and looking after her father. Not much coming back her way.

Her mouth twisted into a mocking grimace as she added, "And sex doesn't fill that space. It never will."

It shamed him, made him realise how blinded he'd been by his own desire for her, blinded every which way from his initial prejudice against her job with his grandmother to her physical response to the sexual attraction between them.

"Please…will you let me go now?"

What could he do?

He stepped back and let her go, watching the doors slide shut, knowing there was nothing he could say that would change her mind about him. No power in the world would force her to see him differently, not at this point. Besides, it was plain she wanted what he was not prepared to give.

Love…marriage…family.

It was not on his agenda.

But he hated leaving her…so empty.

It made him feel empty himself.

CHAPTER FOURTEEN

ISABELLA VALERI KING sighed in contentment and smiled at her long-trusted confidante. "What a splendid night, Rosita!"

They were comfortably seated in armchairs in a corner at the back of the function room. The band's music was not so loud here and it was possible to converse without shouting. On the table in front of them was a selection of sweets—little fruit tarts, cheesecake, apple slices, florentines—which Rosita was sampling one by one, checking out the quality of the catering.

"Everything is good," came the ready agreement. Rosita's dark eyes twinkled. "But I'm thinking you're especially pleased by the absence of people rather than the presence of people."

Isabella allowed herself a smug little smile. "Matteo is definitely taking the initiative. He made himself Nicole's escort tonight, and from my observation before they left this room, they are very caught up with each other."

"The history may suffer," Rosita archly remarked. "When Matteo decides on something he does not let the grass grow under his feet. Nicole will be distracted."

"I would rather have a another good milestone in our

137

family to write about, Rosita. The words can be written when all is resolved.''

''You are so sure they will be right together?''

''Did you not see the way they looked at each other when Nicole was coming down the stairs to the lobby?''

''I saw that she looked very striking, very beautiful. Any man would admire her.''

''No. It was more than that. I am certain of it.''

''Then let us hope it is so. She is too much alone, that one. And immersing herself in other people's lives...'' A sad shake of the head. ''She should have a life of her own. A husband. Babies.''

Isabella couldn't agree more. And Nicole was perfect for Matteo, very strong in her own right, but with much love to give and a sense of loyalty that ran very deep, a woman who would always stand by her man through any hardship.

Her gaze skimmed around the crowd, picking out her other two grandsons and their wives—two couples glowing with happiness. A sense of triumph warmed her heart. If Matteo married Nicole...

There she was!

Isabella sat very upright in her armchair, her back stiffening at a most unwelcome sight.

Nicole was alone.

Where was Matteo?

Most of the people who were not seated as she and Rosita were, had drifted towards the dance floor, either standing in groups around it or gyrating on it in their modern way. Nicole had obviously just re-entered the function room and was in open view as her gaze anxiously searched the more crowded area.

Looking for Matteo?

He was not here.

She looked stressed. Her hands were fretting at the small evening bag she held in front of her at waist level. This was not right to Isabella's mind. What had happened to put Nicole in such a state? Where was Matteo?

"Rosita…" Isabella grasped her arm to draw her attention to Nicole. "…things are not going as they should. Quickly now. Pretend you are going to the powder room. As you pass by Nicole, direct her to me."

"It is not good to meddle," she protested.

"Go! Go!" Isabella commanded, out of patience with holding back and not knowing what was wrong.

Rosita heaved herself up and made her rather ponderous way across the room. Isabella composed herself, hiding her chagrin and making sure an inviting smile was hovering on her lips. Nicole gave Rosita a nervous acknowledgment, too uptight to manage the usual warmth between them. Rosita played her part well, a wave of her arm forcing Nicole to look at Isabella who instantly applied the smile, forcing her wish to talk. As her employee, Nicole would feel bound to oblige, whatever her private inclinations were.

Isabella felt no guilt whatsoever about flexing her power as she watched the young woman tread a slow and reluctant path to pay her respect. It was important to know what was going on now. The tension she had noted between Matteo and Nicole at the theatre should have eased. They had seemed very much together once they'd arrived at the party, clearly attuned to each other.

How long had they been out of the function room? Twenty minutes? Half an hour? Some conflict must have erupted between them. Who was at fault? Could it be fixed? Time for a more propitious encounter was running out tonight and if barriers were set in place again…oh, this was so frustrating!

"Mrs. King…" Nicole greeted her in a flat voice.

Isabella patted the armrest of the vacated chair. "Come sit with me while Rosita's gone," she invited, thinking that time limit shouldn't strain Nicole's nerves too much and any other choice of action would seem impolite.

She moved around the table and sat down without any attempt at small talk. The passive obedience worried Isabella all the more. "I thought Matteo was looking after you tonight," she probed, keeping her tone lightly interested.

Nicole visibly bridled. "He was with me earlier," she said in a corrective tone, glancing around the room again to evade looking directly at Isabella. "I don't know where he is now."

"Didn't I see you leave the party together?"

"We…parted. I went to the powder room."

"How very ungallant of him not to have waited for you! I must speak to that boy."

Red splotches on her cheeks. "It's not his job to look after me, Mrs. King, and I certainly don't want him to feel obliged to do so.'' A low ferocity underlined those words.

Pride, Isabella thought. She frowned for Nicole's benefit. ''You don't like my youngest grandson? Matteo has done something to offend you?''

Instant agitation. ''Please don't think that. It was… kind of him to escort me to and from the theatre. Perhaps he wanted an early night. I am perfectly happy by myself, Mrs. King.''

Perfectly miserable!

''He should not have deserted you,'' she pressed.

''He didn't. Really…'' Pleading eyes begging her to desist. ''…your grandson is free to do whatever he wishes. Just as I am.''

Free…

Freedom was highly overrated in Isabella's opinion. There was Matteo going off doing ridiculously dangerous things like whitewater rafting and bungy-jumping because he didn't have the responsibility of a wife and family. As for Nicole, what was she free for? Books and more books?

She wished she could knock their heads together, get some sense into them. It was clear they had come to the parting of the ways, and Isabella was so annoyed by it, she threw discretion to the winds and bored straight into the heart of the matter.

''I do not like this. I have been aware for some time there is friction between you and Matteo. You were unhappy after your visit to Kauri Pine Park and you have made a point of evading his company since.''

This observation startled Nicole but she bit her lips, offering no comment.

"This cannot be pleasant for you, given your situation in our family circle," Isabella went on. "I was hoping it would sort itself out tonight. If it hasn't, Nicole, I feel bound to step in and..."

"No! There is nothing..." Her eyes flashed a wild vehemence. "...nothing between us." Realising that statement didn't answer the questions raised, she hastily added, "There were...differences...which we've cleared. Truly...there is no need for you to say anything, Mrs. King. I'm sorry that you've been worried."

"So everything is fine now?"

Nicole hesitated, hunting for words that would paper over the problem. "We both know where we stand. That makes it easier."

"There was a misunderstanding?"

"Yes. But no more. So it's all right. Truly."

She jerked her focus away from Isabella, fastening her gaze on the crowd around the dance floor. The agitated dismissal of all concern made it too unkind to continue probing. Indeed, Isabella was allowed no time for it.

"There's Peter!" Nicole cried, leaping to her feet. She shot a pleading glance at Isabella. "Please excuse me, Mrs. King. He said he'd dance with me and I'd like to spend some time with him."

"Of course." She managed a benevolent smile. "Go and enjoy yourself."

"Thank you." Intense relief.

Isabella shook her head as she watched Nicole make

her way to Peter Owen's side. Matteo was a fool to let this woman go. There was Peter welcoming her company, only too happy to draw her onto the dance floor and give her whatever pleasure she sought with him.

Disheartened by the talk which had revealed, at best, that Nicole and Matteo had established a neutral zone; at worst, they were poles apart in what they wanted from each other. But *the wanting* was very real. Nicole would not be so distressed if it wasn't. As for Matteo…where was he? Why was he turning his back on *the wanting* that had pulled Nicole out of this room with him?

Totally exasperated with the situation and wanting to discuss her thoughts on it, Isabella looked to see if Rosita was on her way back from the powder room. Her heart skipped a beat as her gaze found Matteo standing just inside the entrance to the function room, his face tight as though it had just been soundly smacked, his eyes projecting a glowering intensity as they watched the occupants of the dance floor, notably Peter and Nicole, no doubt.

His hands clenched.

But he didn't move to get closer or cut in on Peter.

In two minds about what his next action should be? Isabella wondered.

Rosita appeared behind him. Isabella instantly signalled for her to grab Matteo and bring him over to her. Rosita heaved a reproachful sigh but went ahead and touched his arm to draw his attention. Matteo turned a frown on her, then cleared his face as he saw who it was. They conversed for a few moments. Rosita gestured towards their table and Isabella gave her grandson a bright look of expectation, which sealed his reluctant acquiescence as deftly as she had sealed Nicole's.

He hooked Rosita's arm around his and escorted her back to her chair, acting the gentleman Isabella had trained him to be. "Nonna…" He nodded to her. "…I take it you're still enjoying yourself? Not ready to retire yet?"

"Such wonderful nights do not come very often, Matteo. At my age, who knows how many more I will have?" Which was a fine piece of emotional blackmail. She smiled an appeal. "Do draw up another chair and share a few minutes with me."

A slight wince as he bowed to her pressure, taking a chair from another table and placing it next to hers. He dropped into it with an air of resignation. He aimed a dry smile at Rosita. "Fine selection of sweets you've got on the table in front of you."

"Help yourself, Matteo," she invited effusively. "The cheesecake is very good."

"No, thanks. Not hungry. I'm glad you're enjoying them."

"And you, Matteo?" Isabella broke in. "Have you been enjoying yourself?"

He shrugged. "The show was great. Certainly a night to celebrate."

"Perhaps you would like to dance now. Am I keeping you from it?"

"It can wait," he answered in a careless tone.

Isabella put the needle in. "I see Nicole dancing with

Peter. It must be nice for her to renew their old acquaintance."

"No doubt. A shared background is always congenial."

Was that the problem? He'd read *Ollie's Drum*. Did he think Nicole's background precluded her from making a life up here? Didn't he know that if a love was strong enough, place didn't matter? Her own mother had sailed halfway around the world to be with her father in a very foreign land. She herself would have gone to the Kimberly Outback if her husband had survived the war. Was Matteo nursing some woolly-headed prejudice?

"I do not think those memories are ones Nicole cherishes," she said. "They were hard years for her. She has said many times how much she likes the life around Port Douglas. I think she may stay after she finishes the project."

"Doing what?" came the mocking question. "She's bound to head back to Sydney once her contract is over. There's nothing for her up here."

"What is in Sydney for her?" Isabella countered. "She has no family to draw her back. No permanent home. Nicole plans to take time off and try her hand at writing fiction. One can write anywhere, Matteo."

He frowned and muttered, "The heat will get to her. Six months in the tropics will be long enough for the novelty to wear off."

"Many people love the tropical climate. Look at Hannah. She was from Sydney."

"Hannah doesn't have red hair and white skin," he retorted tersely.

Isabella looked at him in astonishment. "What has that got to do with anything?"

He grimaced and made a sharp, dismissive gesture. "Nicole will get burnt. Or suffer sunstroke. She's obviously not suited to…"

"You've met the King family from the Kimberly," Isabella cut in, exasperated by this superficial judgment. "Tommy King's wife, Samantha, has carrot-red hair and very fair skin. She was born and bred in the Outback, with heat and sun that's even more blistering than what we get in Port Douglas."

"That's always been her life," he argued.

"And you think Nicole Redman can't manage it?" Isabella tossed back, barely able to keep the scorn from her voice. "Didn't you say you'd read her book about her father, Matteo?"

"Yes, I did," he snapped, not wanting to be reminded of it.

"Then didn't it occur to you that Nicole is a survivor?" Isabella bored in, relentless in her mission to pull the wool from her blind grandson's eyes. "Given some of the worst circumstances a child could face, that girl came through everything with a strength I can only admire. With a grit and determination that would have served some of the leaders in this country well. With amazing and fearless enterprise, she coped with enormous difficulties and…"

"In my opinion, she wasted her young life on a man

who didn't deserve what she did for him," Matteo
flashed at her, a black resentment in his eyes.

"He was her father," Isabella retorted, outraged by
this view. "Would you not have rescued your own father
if you could have done so?"

"Yes, I would have braved the cyclone that killed him
if I'd been anywhere near him, but…"

"A child does not think of the cost to themselves. We
are talking blood family here. Sticking to family. It is a
quality all too lacking in modern day society. It is a
quality I value very highly. I am disappointed that you
do not, Matteo."

"Nonna…" Sheer fury looked at her. He jerked his
head away, took a deep breath, expelled it slowly, then
rose to his feet and looked down at her with hooded
eyes. "I really don't wish to discuss Nicole Redman any
further," he stated flatly. "I have an early flight in the
morning so please excuse me. Goodnight, Nonna…
Rosita…"

He strode off with stiff-necked pride, not glancing at
the dance floor, intent on denying any interest whatsoever in Nicole Redman. But Isabella was not in any
doubt that he had been trying to justify a view which he
was using as an excuse not to commit himself to a serious relationship with Nicole. Why he wanted an excuse
was beyond her.

Did *freedom* mean so much to him?

"He is very angry," Rosita murmured.

Isabella sighed. "I lost my temper." She turned to her

old friend. "But have you ever heard such nonsense, Rosita?"

She made one of her very expressive Italian gestures. "I think he is hurting badly but he doesn't like to say so. Matteo has always been like that. He jokes to make little of things that hurt."

"He wasn't joking tonight."

"Which means it is a very bad hurt."

"They are both hurting." Isabella shook her head worriedly. "The question is…can they get past it? I may have smashed the barriers in Matteo's mind tonight, but is he prepared to smash the barriers he put in Nicole's?" Her eyes flared her deep frustration. "That is beyond my power. Only Matteo can do it, Rosita. Only he…if he wants to enough."

CHAPTER FIFTEEN

PREGNANT!

Oh, God! Oh, God! Oh, God!

What was she to do?

With shaking hands, Nicole piled all the evidence of the pregnancy test into a plastic bag to dispose of somewhere away from the castle when she felt up to a walk. She couldn't leave it lying around for Rosita to find. The motherly Italian housekeeper was very thorough in her cleaning.

Still in shock, Nicole tottered from her ensuite bathroom, stowed the incriminating packaging in her straw carry-bag, then crawled onto her bed and buried her face in a pillow. It was Sunday morning. She was not expected to work on Sundays. It didn't matter if she was late down for breakfast. In fact, Sunday was a good excuse to miss it altogether. Even the thought of food sickened her, especially first thing in the morning.

Now she knew why.

The punishment for her madness with Matt King.

She couldn't even blame him, knowing she'd been equally responsible. Though *irresponsible* was the correct word. Wild stupid recklessness, not even thinking of the possibility of getting pregnant. Only when she'd gone to bed—alone—after the premiere party had she wondered and worried, and decided there was a good chance she was safe. It simply wouldn't be fair to end up paying even more than the intense emotional letdown from that one experience.

A baby.

No more hiding her head in the sand, finding excuses for her period to be late—the heat, stress, anything but the truth. The truth had just stared her in the face. She was undeniably pregnant. And somehow she now had to plan a future with a baby…a child…a child of her own.

She vividly recalled Matt King spouting off about the responsibilities of fatherhood, but did she want him to be connected to her and their child for the rest of their lives? A man who'd only wanted sex with her? A man who raised turbulent feelings every time she saw him?

Only a few days ago he had dropped in at the castle, stopping to join his grandmother for afternoon tea. He'd breezed out to the loggia where Nicole had been sitting with her employer, cheerfully announcing, "I just left a box of exotic fruit with Rosita in the kitchen." Then with a dazzling grin aimed at her, he'd added, "I brought some mangosteen especially for you, Nicole. It was your favourite, wasn't it?"

"Yes. Thank you," she'd managed to get out as she'd tried to quell the flush erupting from his reminder of their fruit-tasting.

Luckily he'd chatted to his grandmother for a while, giving her time to adjust to his presence. Not that it helped much. Her mind kept fretting over why he'd come and the mention of the fruit seemed like an indication that he still wanted sex with her. Was he scouting his chances?

She'd kept her eyes downcast. It was disturbing enough, hearing his voice, feeling his energy swirling around her. When he'd asked about her progress on the family history, forcing her to look at him, she'd had to concentrate very hard on giving appropriate replies. He'd been quite charming about it, not critical at all, no dubious comments, yet his half-hour visit had left her completely drained.

Even if he remained simply polite to her, she didn't want to be near him. It was too much of a strain, fighting his sexual attraction. And she certainly didn't want him to feel honour-bound to offer marriage because of becoming an accidental father. That would be totally humiliating, knowing he hadn't considered her in the light of a possible wife for him.

No love.

At least, by having a baby, her life wouldn't be empty of love anymore. That was one positive to comfort her. Though how she would manage as a single mother…she would have to start thinking about it, planning.

Four hours later, Nicole was feeling considerably better. She'd walked down to the marina, got rid of the pregnancy test in a large waste bin, idled away some time watching activity on the boats, wandered around the market stalls set up in Anzac Park, lingering at those offering baby clothes and toys, finally buying a gift for Hannah's baby, telling herself it was far too soon to start acquiring anything for her own. Better to wait until she was settled somewhere.

Not here in Port Douglas.

She couldn't live anywhere near Matt King.

The rest of his family she liked very much. Alex and Gina had taken an apartment in Brisbane for the duration of the show, with Alex commuting to Port Douglas as business demanded. Mrs. King missed having them close, especially the children, but today Tony and Hannah had come to lunch at the castle and their company always cheered her.

Usually Nicole enjoyed being with them, too. They were happy people. But today, as they sat around a table near the fountain in the loggia, their happiness made her feel sad. This is how it should be, she kept thinking, a man and a woman loving each other, getting married, having a baby because they both wanted it. Hannah seemed to glow with good health. Nicole wondered if she had suffered morning sickness earlier on in her pregnancy, but she couldn't ask.

"Matt!"

Tony's cry of surprise sent a shock through her heart. Her head dizzied as her gaze jerked to the man coming out of the castle, brandishing cutlery and serviette.

"Knew you'd be here, Tony, so I thought I'd join you," he announced. "Rosita said you were lunching outside so I've come armed for the feast."

"There's such a nice breeze," Hannah explained. "We didn't want to be inside."

"Good thinking," Matt approved. "I'll just move you

up a place, Hannah, so I can sit next to Nonna.'' He smiled at his grandmother. "I trust I'm welcome?''

She returned his smile. "Always, Matteo.''

"Nicole...'' He nodded to her as he rearranged the seating. "...how are you?''

"Fine, thank you,'' she managed to reply, though her stomach was now in knots.

He was seating himself almost directly opposite her, which meant she'd be facing him all through lunch, the man who'd fathered a child with her and didn't know it.

Fortunately, Tony claimed his brother's attention, chatting on about the tourist business which was of vital interest to both of them. They were coming out of the wet season, which meant the influx of visitors to Port Douglas was rapidly increasing, people wanting a vacation in the sun and trips to the Great Barrier Reef and other wonders of the tropical far north.

Rosita wheeled out a traymobile loaded with a variety of salads and a huge coral trout that she'd baked with a herb and pinenut crust. She placed the platter containing the fish in front of Tony to carve into servings and the smell of the herbs wafted down the table, instantly making Nicole feel nauseous. Trying to counter the effect, she sipped her iced juice, desperately breathing in the scent of its tropical fruit.

"Only a very small portion for me please, Tony,'' she requested when he was about to serve her.

"Don't stint yourself because I'm an unexpected guest,'' Matt quickly threw in, his gaze targeting her with persuasive intent. "There's more than enough to go around."

"I'm not really hungry," she excused, savagely wishing he wouldn't look directly at her. He was so wickedly handsome, it screwed up her heart, making it hop, skip and jump in a highly erratic fashion.

"But you missed breakfast this morning," Mrs. King remarked, surprised by Nicole's lack of appetite.

She sought wildly for a reasonable explanation. "While I was wandering around the market stalls…"

"You succumbed to the famous prawn sandwich?" Matt supplied, his brilliant dark eyes twinkling teasingly.

She nodded, robbed of speech. He was putting out magnetic sex appeal again, reducing her to a quivering mess inside. Thankfully Hannah rescued her.

"And look what she bought the baby at the markets, Matt!" She leaned down beside her chair, took the cleverly crafted caterpillar from the plastic bag and demonstrated how the multi-coloured segments could be stretched out and when released, they'd bunch together again. "Isn't it gorgeous?"

Hannah was beaming pleasure at her brother-in-law and he beamed pleasure right back at her. "Fantastic! I can see little hands having a fun time with that."

Tears pricked Nicole's eyes at the thought of her own baby's little hands, reaching out for a father who wasn't there, a father who'd never watch him or her having fun.

"Well bought, Nicole," Matt declared with warm approval, turning her to absolute mush.

Why was he doing this?

Why was he here?

Hadn't she made it clear that she would not have an affair with him? She wanted what Tony and Hannah had, not just a physical thing that went nowhere but bed.

Distractedly she helped herself to salads, hoping to smother the herb smell on the plate Tony had passed to her. The result was a heap of food she couldn't possibly eat, which made her feel even worse. She picked up her knife and fork, telling herself she had to get through this, had to act normally and not draw any attention to her state of helpless torment.

"Did you try one of the exotic fruit ices while you were down in Anzac Park?" Matt asked her, forcing further conversation with him.

Nicole gave him a fleeting glance as she answered, "No, I didn't."

"Then you missed out on a treat," he cheerfully persisted. "They're very flavoursome and refreshing. The people who run the stall buy their fruit from me. They do well with it."

Wishing she could ignore him but knowing it would be perceived as impolite by Mrs. King, Nicole forced her gaze up from her plate and managed a quick smile. "I'm sure they do. I did notice they had quite long queues at that stall, people waiting to be served."

Her eyes didn't quite meet his but only he would notice, and hopefully he would get the message that she wasn't interested and would prefer to be left alone. She picked doggedly at the salads she'd chosen, determined on closing him out as much as she could. He chatted to his grandmother, apparently not having noticed anything untoward in Nicole's behaviour. It was as though he wasn't aware of any tension, or was consciously ignoring it, hoping it would go away.

It didn't go away for Nicole. She had the strong sense of Matt King biding his time, waiting to pounce when the opportunity presented itself, planning how to manoeuvre her away from the others. He'd given no notice of his coming and his arrival had coincided with the serving of lunch, which meant she couldn't easily absent herself. She was sure this was planned, not an impulse. Behind it all was a relentless will beating at her, not letting go.

It made her head ache. Her stomach started to revolt against the food she was doing her best to eat. She sipped her juice, desperate to control the waves of nausea. It was no use. The added stress of Matt King's presence was just too much to bear on top of everything else. The casual cheerfulness of his voice, the confident way he was dealing with his meal, the sheer power of the man…it all made her feel weak and miserable.

She set down her cutlery, placed her serviette by her plate and pushed up from her chair. ''Please excuse me.'' She swept an apologetic look around the table, then directly addressed her employer. ''I must have walked too long in the heat this morning.'' She rubbed her forehead which was definitely clammy. ''I'm just not well.''

Mrs. King frowned in concern. ''Go and lie down, my dear. I'll check on you later.''

"Thank you."

"If it's an upset stomach, could be the prawn sandwich," Hannah suggested as Nicole made her way around the table. "Takeaway food can be tricky."

"Yes," Nicole agreed weakly.

"Or is it sunstroke?" Matt queried. "Do you feel feverish, Nicole?"

"Only a headache," she answered, wishing they'd just let her go without fuss, fixing her gaze on the double entrance doors to the castle to deflect any further inquiries about her health.

A chair scraped on the cobblestones. Matt spoke, *not letting her go.* "I'll accompany you up to your room. Make sure you're all right."

"No!"

She spun to face the man she most wanted to escape, her hand flying out in a warding-off protest. He was on his feet, so big and tall he seemed to tower over her, filling her vision with multiple images. Which was wrong. She was dizzy from having whirled on him so fast, the shock of his action draining the blood from her face.

The next thing she knew was finding herself clamped to Matt King's chest, then being set in his chair, head down between her knees, his arm around her supportively, his voice ringing in her ears as he crouched to her level.

"Deep breaths. Get some oxygen back in your brain."

Had she fainted?

Embarrassment churned through her. Having so much

attention focused on her was dreadful. "I'm all right," she gasped, intensely distressed at having made this spectacle of herself.

"You were blacking out, Nicole. Take your time now," Matt advised. He felt her forehead. "Not overly hot. A bit clammy."

"Perhaps I should call a doctor," Mrs. King said worriedly.

"No!" Nicole cried, alarmed by what a doctor might tell her employer. She had to keep the pregnancy a secret. "I just need to lie down for a while. Truly…"

"I'll carry her up to her room, Nonna. Make sure she's okay," Matt said.

"You do that, Matteo, and I'll go and speak to Rosita. She has remedies for everything."

"Oh, please…" Nicole barely got those words out before she was lifted off the chair and cradled across the same broad masculine chest she had struggled against at the Brisbane hotel.

"I'll get the doors open for you," Tony chimed in, already out of his chair and striding ahead of them.

Fighting them all seemed like fighting an unstoppable juggernaut. Nicole felt too weak to do it. She let herself be carried into the castle, hating the enforced awareness of the man who was carrying her, his strength, the sense of once more being enveloped by him. She refused to put her arms around his neck to make the carrying easier. It would bring her into even closer contact with him, possibly encouraging whatever devious plan he had in mind.

Tony didn't follow them in. Mrs. King left them at the staircase, pursuing her own path to the kitchen and Rosita. This left Nicole alone with Matt King as he started up the stairs.

"Put me down. I can walk," she pleaded.

"It's not far. I can manage," he stated firmly, as though she was worrying about being too heavy a burden.

She closed her eyes and took a deep breath, which was a mistake because she breathed in the warm male scent of him and her head swam again. "Why are you doing this?" she hissed, angry at her own vulnerability to an attraction she didn't want to feel.

"You need help."

"I don't want you holding me."

"You surely don't imagine I'm taking you up to your bedroom to seduce you when you're obviously sick."

She was too agitated to think straight.

"Seduction wasn't what we were about anyway," he added dryly. "You know that, Nicole."

"I'm not going to change my mind," she blurted out, desperate for him to understand her position.

"I didn't expect you to."

"Then why are you here?"

"Was I supposed to be banned from the castle?"

She floundered, knowing it was absurd to try to cut him off from his grandmother for the duration of the project. "You know what I mean," she muttered helplessly.

"You wanted enough notice so you could avoid me?"

She bit her lips, knowing to concede that also conceded how deeply he affected her. But he knew it already, she wildly reasoned. Nothing would have happened between them if she hadn't wanted it to.

"You made your point, Nicole," he went on quietly. "I'm not going to push anything else."

He didn't have to, she thought miserably. She was a mess around him anyway. He'd reached the top of the staircase, seemingly without any effort at all, and headed down the corridor towards the guest suites.

"Which door?" he asked.

"Please...put me down now," she begged. "I'll be fine. The dizziness has gone."

"Which door?" he repeated.

"I don't want you coming into my private room," she cried. "It's *private*... to *me!*"

He stopped. His chest rose as he sucked in a deep breath and fell as he expelled it. Slowly, carefully, he set her on her feet, still holding her as he waited to see if she really was steady enough to be safely released.

"I was only trying to look after you, Nicole, not take some...some crass advantage," he said quietly. "I'm sorry I left you thinking so badly of me. Next time we meet..." Another deep sigh. "There's no need for you to feel stressed in my company. Okay?"

"Yes. Thank you. May I go now?" she rushed out, unable to look at him with tears pricking her eyes again.

"As you wish," he murmured, dropping his hands.

She made it to her room in a blind dash, conscious he was waiting, watching. It was an enormous relief to close the door on him. She stood against it, letting the tears roll, swallowing the sobs that threatened to erupt.

Trying to look after her...

I want someone to care about me. Look after me.

Those were the words she'd hurled at him in the elevator. Did he remember them or was he just reacting to her being ill in front of his family? Nothing really personal. Except he wanted to call at the castle without her being stressed. Which was totally impossible now she was pregnant with his child.

Oh, God! Oh, God! Oh, God!

What was she to do?

CHAPTER SIXTEEN

ISABELLA VALERI KING decided this was no time for sensitivities. There was very little time left for anything. If she was wrong, Matteo could soon set her right. However, if the situation was what she suspected it to be, action had to be taken before Nicole drove back to Sydney. Once in her home city, it would be all too easy for an enterprising and determined woman to make herself uncontactable in any direct sense.

The contract to write the family history would not be broken. Isabella had no doubt about Nicole's integrity on that promise. The research had been thorough with everything recorded for easy reference. The argument that the writing could be done anywhere was irrefutable. Nicole Redman was going and Isabella knew in her heart there'd be no coming back to Port Douglas. An irrevocable decision had been made.

Unless Matteo stopped it.

If he had reason to stop it.

With all this churning through her mind, Isabella entered the KingTours main office, intent on a face-to-face confrontation with her youngest grandson.

"Mrs. King!" the boy behind the desk cried in surprise, this being a rare and unheralded visitation by a woman of legendary stature in the community.

"Is my grandson in his office?" she demanded. He ought to be. It was Friday morning. And she didn't want to hear any excuses for not meeting with her.

"Yes," the boy informed, not seeing any reason to check with his employer.

"Good! You need not announce me," she instructed, leaving him staring after her as she marched into Matteo's office and closed the door firmly behind her.

Matteo looked up from the paperwork on his desk with the same air of stunned surprise. "Nonna! What are you doing here?"

She paused, for the first time wondering if she was about to do him an injustice. Giving herself more time to think, she moved slowly to the vacant chair on this side of his desk and sat down.

"Is something wrong?" he asked in quick concern, rising from his chair.

She held up a hand to stop him. "I only wish to talk, Matteo."

He frowned, sinking back onto his seat. "What about?"

"It's Friday. I thought perhaps you might intend to visit me this afternoon."

He nodded, his brow still creased, more in puzzlement now. "I had planned to drop by. Is there a problem?"

"Nicole is leaving us. She begins the long drive back to Sydney tomorrow."

His frown deepened again. "Do you mean she is breaking her contract with you?"

"No. She will write the family history. But she will not remain at the castle to do so."

"Did she give a reason?"

"She says the heat is getting to her. And it is true that she has been unwell all this week."

He grimaced. "I did say…"

"It is nonsense, Matteo," Isabella cut in. "She has been here three months, through the hottest time of the year, with no ill effect whatsoever. Until very recently."

"Last Sunday…"

"Yes. That was the most noticeable."

"Since then?"

"She has not been…herself."

"Maybe the heat has gradually worn her down, Nonna."

"No. It is not logical."

His eyes narrowed. "So what do you think? Why come to me?" he rapped out.

"I may be old but I'm not blind, Matteo. There has been something between you and Nicole. She is tense in your presence and you are certainly not indifferent to her."

"Are you blaming *me* for this choice she's made?" he challenged tersely.

"Are you to blame?" she fired straight at him.

His hands lifted in an impatient gesture. "I have tried to put Nicole more at ease with me. If she cannot accept that…"

"Maybe it is not possible, Matteo," Isabella said sadly. "Rosita says Nicole is pregnant."

''What?''

His shock was patent.

Again Isabella paused, not certain that he was responsible. She sat silently, watching him deal with what was obviously news to him.

He shook his head incredulously. Then his face tightened as though he'd been hit by some truth he recognised. He shot an intense look at her. ''How does Rosita know this?''

Isabella shrugged. ''I have never known Rosita to be wrong on the matter of pregnancy. She says there is a look about a woman. She told me Hannah was pregnant weeks before Antonio announced it. I don't doubt Rosita's judgment, Matteo. And as much as Nicole tries to hide it, her morning sickness...''

''She's been sick every morning?''

''For over a week now.''

''Before last Sunday?''

''Yes.''

Clenched fists crashed down on the desk. ''She knew.'' He erupted from his chair. ''She knew!'' He paced around the desk, his hands flying out in violent agitation. ''Why didn't she tell me? She had the chance.''

All doubt was now erased. Isabella took a deep breath and said, ''Nicole must have felt she had good reason not to tell you, Matteo.''

''But...'' He sliced the air in angry dismissal. ''...I told her how I feel about fatherhood.''

"How *you* feel. Perhaps you should consider how Nicole feels."

"It's my child!" he protested. "She can't just ignore that, Nonna."

"If you want any part in your child's life, I advise you to proceed with great care, Matteo. With great care."

She stood with all the dignity at her command, bringing to a halt the wild tempest of energy emanating from her grandson.

"In this matter Nicole has all the rights," she said to sober him. "And if she leaves tomorrow, your child will be gone with her. This is not a time for rash action or anger, Matteo. It is a time for caring, for kindness, for understanding."

She walked to the door. Matteo did not move to open it for her. She looked back at him, saw conflict raging across his face, tension gripping his entire body, the need to act almost explosive.

Was this turbulence they struck in each other the cause of all the problems?

Isabella shook her head.

What more could she do?

"It is not the heat nor the pregnancy that has made Nicole Redman sick to her soul," she said sadly. "You would do well to think on that today, Matteo. Whatever you decide to do…you will live with this for the rest of your life."

She opened the door and left him.

The decisions were his now.

She could only hope he made the right ones.

CHAPTER SEVENTEEN

EVEN at the last moment, Nicole hesitated, the sealed and addressed envelope still clamped between her finger and thumb as it hovered over the slot in the postal box. It had to be done, she told herself. It wasn't right to deny Matt King knowledge of a child he'd fathered. By the time he received the letter she'd be long gone, although once the baby was born, she would notify him again. Then if he wanted contact…their child had the right to know its father.

That was the really important truth.

She could not turn her back on her child's rights.

Whatever happened with Matt King in the future she would learn to cope with it…somehow. This had to be done. Her finger and thumb lifted apart. The envelope dropped.

Nicole hurried back to her car. No turning back on this course now. All week she had fretted over it. A weight seemed to shift from her shoulders as she settled herself in the driver's seat. There was nothing more that had to be done.

It was almost five o'clock. She'd bought a packet of barley sugar to suck on the trip tomorrow in the hope it would keep any sickness at bay, plus bottles of mineral water to stop dehydration. Only one more night at the castle…

She drove around the town one last time, knowing she would miss this place, wanting to remember everything about it. Maybe, sometime in the future, her child would come here for visits, if Matt King wanted that. It was a heart-wrenching thought. Tears pricked her eyes. She blinked them away and drove up to the castle, wanting to catch the sunset from the tower.

Rosita was in the kitchen when Nicole carried in the bottles of water to put in the refrigerator overnight. "I have made my special lasagna for your dinner," the motherly housekeeper announced.

Nicole didn't feel like eating anything heavy but she smiled, knowing Rosita wanted to give her a last treat. "I'm sure I'll enjoy it."

"I will pack a picnic box for you to take in the morning." Her kind eyes searched Nicole's in hopeful concern. "Is there anything else I can do for you?"

"No, thank you, Rosita. You've been marvellous to me. I'm just going up to the tower now to watch the sunset."

"Ah, yes. It is a fine view from the tower. Take care not to fall on the steps. They are very old and worn."

Nicole took away the strong impression that Rosita knew what she'd tried to keep hidden. Or at least suspected it. All the fussing over her, the admonitions to *take care*… but nothing had been said. Sadness dragged on her heart as she climbed the steps to the tower. She would miss Rosita's motherliness. Having been motherless for so many years, it had been nice to be fussed over, cared about.

There was so much she would miss.

Many times she had come up here to the topmost level of the castle, having finished work for the day and needing a relaxing break before dinner. The view was fantastic to every horizon, the sea, the mountains, the endless sky, all the colours beginning to change as the sun lowered.

She walked around the tessellated wall, taking in the many vistas one last time, stopping finally at her favourite view over Dickenson Inlet where the boats came into the marina, the cane fields on the other side of it stretching out to sea, and beyond them the darkening hills behind which the sun would sink.

It was so calming, peaceful, beautiful. She thought of her employer's mother, Marguerita Valeri, standing here in the old days, watching the ships come in from the sea, watching the cane fields burn at harvest time, watching the sun set, and for the first time it occurred to Nicole that her child—Matt King's child—was part of the same pioneering bloodline that had built this castle and so much else up here in the far north.

She herself might never belong anywhere but her child had deep family roots. A real history. A history she would write so it would always be known. It was something good she could give. And maybe Matt—if he truly felt the responsibilities of fatherhood—would provide their child with a solid sense of belonging.

*   *   *

Matt reached the top of the tower and halted, gathering himself to do what had to be done. Nicole was standing at the far wall, her back turned to him, her gaze seemingly fixed on the view his grandmother liked best. Her tall slender figure was completely still, wrapped in a loneliness he knew he had to break.

The setting sun gave the frame of her fiery hair a glowing aura. The shining of inner strength, he thought, though the rest of her looked fragile. The urge to simply take her in his arms was strong, but he sternly reminded himself that taking was not keeping and Nicole would resist force.

Only the truth would serve him now.

His anger at her keeping everything to herself had dissipated hours ago. His pride was worth nothing in the face of losing this woman and the child she was carrying. If Rosita was right about the pregnancy, he had to win both of them. He had to reach Nicole with the truth, make it speak for him, make it count.

One chance.

He couldn't afford to mess it up.

Matt took a deep, deep breath and called to her.

"Nicole…"

Her heart leapt.

His voice.

She turned with a sense of disbelief, having already relegated him to the past, and the far future. He wasn't supposed to appear in the here and now. Yet he was striding towards her, large as life, the force of his vital energy making her pulse flutter and spreading a buzz of confusion through her entire body.

"What are you doing here?" she cried, her mind struggling to accept a reality she didn't want to face.

He slowed his step, his hands lifting in an appeal, his dark eyes begging her forbearance. "Sorry if I startled you. I came by after work to see my grandmother. She mentioned you were leaving us tomorrow."

"Yes. Yes, I am. I don't need to stay here to do the writing," she gabbled out, belatedly remembering he worked in the KingTours offices on Fridays and cursing herself for not foreseeing the possibility of a casual visit to the castle. Although why he had to come up here, seeking her out...

"Is it because of me?" he asked, coming to a halt at the tessellated wall right beside her, barely an arm's length away, and turned to face her, an urgent intensity in the eyes searching hers.

Her heart thumped wildly. "Why would you think that? I told Mrs. King..."

"There are more kinds of heat than the weather," he said with savage irony, "and I know I'm guilty of subjecting you to them, Nicole."

He was doing it again right now.

She turned her face to the sunset, hoping the red glow in the sky would somehow hide the tide of heat rushing up her neck, scorching her cheeks. Her mind literally could not come up with a dismissive reply. It was drowning in the truth he'd just spoken, a whirlpool of truth that had swept her around in tormenting circles ever since she had met Matt King.

"I've been very wrong about you," he went on quietly. "And I regret, very deeply, making you feel...threatened by me. I wish I could take it all back and we could start again."

Impossible. What was done couldn't be undone. The new life she carried forced her to move on. And regrets didn't change anything. Though at least his admission of being wrong about her might make a rapprochement between them easier in the future.

"I'm glad you don't think badly of me anymore," she said, steeling herself to look directly at him one more time. "Let's leave it at that."

His gaze locked onto hers with compelling strength. "I can't. I don't want you to go, Nicole."

She shook her head, pained by the raw desire in his eyes, in his voice. Her stomach was curling in protest. She placed her hand over it, instinctively protective. "Please...it's no good."

"It can be good," he argued vehemently. "The two of us together...it *was* good. Better than anything I've known with any other woman."

Sex!

She recoiled from him.

"Wait!" His arm lifted in urgent intent to halt her retreat. "I know I've messed up everything. It was stupid, trying to negate the truth of what I felt, trying to sidetrack it. I didn't want to get...*hooked* on you."

"I'm not...not...*bait!*" she cried, horrified at the image his words conjured up.

"I thought my grandmother..." He broke off, venting a sigh that carried a wealth of exasperation.

"What about your grandmother?"

He grimaced. "Nonna is into matchmaking. She found Gina for Alex, inviting her to the castle as a wedding singer. And she hired Hannah as the cook for Tony's prized catamaran, *Duchess,* putting her right under his nose. I know she wants all three of us married, having families. I thought she'd picked you for me."

She stared at him in total disbelief. "That's...that's crazy!"

Another grimace. "Not as crazy as it sounds."

"You don't think *I* might have a say in whom I marry?"

"I'm trying to explain..." He looked harassed, raking a hand through the tight curls above his ear, frowning, gesturing an appeal for patience. "I wanted her to be wrong. And when I remembered you from New Orleans..."

"You concocted a scenario that put me in the light of a totally unsuitable wife," she hotly accused.

"Yes," he admitted fiercely. "And grabbed at every other reason I could think of, too. Anything to stop me from even thinking of pursuing the attraction I felt. I was pig-headedly determined not to fall into Nonna's marriage trap, even though..." He shook his head self-mockingly. "...she had nothing to do with the attraction I felt for you ten years ago."

"You mean...in New Orleans?" she asked, confused by his previous interpretation of her work there.

"I tagged on to your tour that night, just to watch you, listen to you. If I hadn't been a tourist...if I could have met you in some appropriate way...but my time there was at an end and I told myself it was fantasy."

Amazed at this turnabout in his view of her, she ruefully murmured, "I wouldn't have had time for you anyway."

"Our paths were at cross-purposes, but does it have to be like that now, Nicole?"

Pain washed through her. The cross-purposes couldn't be worse. Pregnancy was the oldest marriage trap in the world. It was too late to simply pursue an attraction to see where it might lead and he'd just made it impossible for her to admit the truth. He didn't want to be *trapped*.

She stared at him, hopelessly torn by the possibility he offered, wishing time could be turned back, wishing it was just the two of them, a man and a woman, free to start out on a promising journey...but it wasn't so. It just wasn't so.

Her silence pressed him into more speech, his eagerness to convince her of his sincerity permeating every word. "When I read your book, I realised what a fool I'd been to even question your integrity and your ability to do anything you set out to do. I hadn't meant to hurt you. I'm sorry I did. Genuinely sorry."

The passion in his voice stormed around her heart, squeezing. She wrenched her gaze from his, afraid of being swayed into clutching at some way to have another chance with him. But the idea of deception was sickening. The truth about her pregnancy would have to come out. No choice at all. And she couldn't bear him to feel bound to her because of their baby. This nerve-tearing impasse had to be ended.

"I forgive you that hurt," she said flatly, staring at the long red streaks in the sky, the bleeding tatters of a dying day. "You don't have to worry about it anymore."

"That night in Brisbane..."

She tensed, instinctively armouring herself against letting that memory invade and undermine her resolution.

"...you wanted me, too, Nicole," he said softly.

"Yes, I did. You have nothing to blame yourself for on that account," she clipped out as coldly as she could.

"Can you forget it?"

It was a biting challenge, determined on getting to her, arousing all the feelings they had shared in the heat of the moment. No cold then. And he wanted to remove the chill now, reminding her...

She closed her eyes, determined on sealing off all vulnerability to him. If she didn't see, didn't feel...

"I can't. I don't think I ever will," he said with skin-prickling conviction. "It was as though we were meant for each other. Perfectly matched. You tapped things in me I've never felt before."

Nicole gritted her teeth. Just sex, she savagely reminded herself. Great sex, admittedly, but still only sex.

"It was like...all of me reaching for all of you...and finding a togetherness which went beyond the merely physical. And because it was so…so incredible…I was impatient to experience it again, not taking the time to…"

"It's okay!" she choked out, unable to bear his recollections. "I didn't anticipate what happened, either. We didn't plan it. We didn't…*choose* it."

In a spurt of almost-frenzied energy she turned on him, desperate to finish it. "That's the one right we hold unassailable in our lives…to choose for ourselves. You didn't want your grandmother's choice thrust upon you. I understand that. And I don't want a…a fling with you."

"That's not what I want, either," he shot back.

"Then what do you want?" she cried helplessly, her hands flapping a frantic protest. "What's all this about? Why try to stop me from leaving?"

"Because I love you!" he retorted vehemently, stunning her, stunning himself with the force of feeling he'd hurled into the maelstrom of need that was tearing at both of them.

They stared at each other, a mountain of emotion churning between them. He scaled it first, charging ahead with all the pent-up ferocity of a warrior committed to battle.

"I just need the time to give you every reason to love me. I know I haven't done that yet, but I will. *I will!*"

Still she couldn't believe her ears. "You…love… me?"

He drew in a deep breath, but his gaze did not waver even slightly from the incredulity in hers. "I do. I love you," he stated again. "You're in my mind, night and day. If you'll just stop pushing me away, I'll show you I can and will look after you, that I do care about the person you are. Whatever your needs are, I'll answer them. I want to answer them."

She stared mutely at him, feeling as though her whole world had just shifted on its axis. "You hardly know me." The words spilled from a swirling abyss of doubts.

"Nicole, I've read parts of your book over and over again." He stepped forward and gently cupped her cheek, his eyes burning into hers as his tenderly stroking fingers burnt into her skin, seeking every path to the torment in her soul. "I love the child who had the courage to lead her father away from the darkness he was in danger of falling into. I love the young woman who gave the end of his life as much meaning as she could. You shine through the whole story…"

"It's not about me," she protested, her voice reduced to a husky whisper.

"It reveals the heart of you. The kind of heart a man would be a fool not to love."

"Maybe…" She swallowed hard, trying to work some moisture into her mouth. "Maybe you…you think that. But feeling it is something different."

"How does this feel?"

He tilted her chin and she was too stunned to take any evasive action before his mouth claimed hers, not with blitzing passion but with a tantalisingly seductive sensuality that wooed her into accepting the kiss, testing it for herself, feeling the electric tingle of his restraint, letting it happen because she needed to know *his* truth beyond any niggle of doubt before she could surrender her own.

"I love you," he murmured, feathering her lips with the feeling words, then drawing back to look into her eyes with mesmerising fervour. "I love everything about you."

He smiled whimsically as his fingers softly nudged her hair behind her ears. "Your hair is like a brilliant beacon calling to me."

A moth to a flame, he'd said before.

His hands trailed down to her shoulders. "I love the way you hold yourself. It shouts—*I am a woman and proud of it.* And so you should be proud of who you are, all you are, Nicole."

I am, she thought, ashamed of nothing, not even the slip in sensible caution that had made her vulnerable to falling pregnant. Maybe it was meant to be because he was *the man,* she thought dizzily, and as though he could read her mind, his next words melted the armour she'd tried to hold around her heart.

"It excites me simply to look at you. It's like all my instincts immediately start clamouring—*this is the woman…the woman for me.* It happens every time I see you, and it's so powerful I have no control over it. You can call it primitive. I don't care. It's there…and I believe it's there for you, too, Nicole."

He shook his head at her, negating any denial she might make. "You wouldn't have let us come together in Brisbane if you didn't feel the same way," he pressed on. "You would have shot me out of your room. It was right for us. It was how it was meant to be between us, and would have been all along if I hadn't put up barriers to keep you at a distance."

Was that true? If she hadn't sensed antagonism in him at their first meeting, if he hadn't been so cynically challenging, if he'd been welcoming, charming...she probably would have fallen in love with him on the spot, dazzled right out of her mind. As it was, she'd resented his sexual impact on her, hated it. Yet when she'd surrendered to the intense desires he stirred, it had felt right, beautifully wonderfully right. Could it be that way again if...but there was still the baby.

"All I'm asking is that you stay on here," he said earnestly. "Let me show you..."

"I'm pregnant!" she blurted out, then instantly averted her gaze from his, frightened of the effect of such a stark statement on his plans for whatever relationship he wanted with her. Only a golden rim of the sun was left shimmering above the dark hills. Twilight hovered above it, a purpling sky that signalled the end of this day. The night would come. And then tomorrow...

"I wrote you a letter. It's posted to KingTours. It says we...we made a baby...when we came together," she said in a desperate rush, needing him to understand the emotional dilemma of a future neither of them had planned or even foreseen. "I would have written again when the baby was born. In case...in case you wanted to be a real father. Like you said..."

Silence.

Silence so fraught she couldn't breathe.

The trap, she thought. He's seeing the trap now.

It was no longer a case of winning her over with a promise of love. It wasn't about today or tomorrow or her staying on at the castle for the last three months of the history project. It was about being bonded by a child for the rest of their lives.

CHAPTER EIGHTEEN

"So it's true. You *are* pregnant."

His words fell strangely on Nicole's ears. She had expected shock. The lack of it was mind-jolting.

"I didn't want to believe you'd go without telling me," he went on, hurt gathering momentum. "Without giving me the chance to…"

"You *knew?*" Her own shock spun her around to face him.

He gestured dismissively as though it didn't matter. "Rosita told my grandmother. She thought I should be informed."

"You knew before you came up here and said all those things to me?" Her voice climbed at the shattering of all she'd wanted to believe.

He frowned at her. "How could you do that? Leaving me *a letter?*"

"You don't have to feel responsible. I don't want you spinning me a whole pack of lies to…"

"A letter!" he thundered, cutting her off. "Letting me know so I could stew about it for the next eight months, wondering how you were, worrying if all was well with the baby, while you took care of everything by yourself, shutting me out of both your lives. Was that the plan?"

"Yes!" she snapped. "I couldn't bear you to feel trapped into something you wouldn't have chosen with me."

"You didn't give me the choice. You chose to give me the hell of being shoved aside. Rendered useless. I wasn't to help you through the pregnancy. I wasn't to be at your side when you gave birth to our child. You were going to cheat me of holding our son or our daughter when it came into this world." He threw up his hands, his whole body expressing a towering rage. "How could you do that? How?"

"It's all about possession to you, isn't it?" she fired back at him, defying his stand on what he considered his paternal rights. "Possession, not love. You didn't want to let me go because you knew I had something you wanted."

"Let you go? Not in a million years." Fierce purpose glared at her. "I'm not taking any more nonsense from you, Nicole Redman. We are going to get married. We're going to get married so fast, it'll put Nonna in a total tailspin getting it arranged in time."

She backed away from him. "You can't make me marry you."

"Give me one good reason why you won't," he challenged, his eyes glittering with wild certainty in his cause.

"No one should marry for the sake of a child. It doesn't work," she cried vehemently.

"Marrying for love does."

"You're just saying that."

"No. Don't speak for me, Nicole."

"You *said* you didn't want to be trapped into marriage."

"I'm walking right into it with my eyes wide open." He stepped towards her. She retreated. He kept coming as he pressed his view. "No trap. This is precisely what I want. My woman. My child. A home we share. A future we make together."

His aggressive confidence came at her like a tidal wave, swallowing up everything in its path, crashing past barriers as though they were nothing. Nicole struggled to hold on to the sense of the decisions she'd made.

"If I hadn't fallen pregnant…"

"You would have stayed at the castle long enough for me to show you we belonged with each other."

"How can I know that?" She stretched out her hands, pleading her uncertainty. "How can I believe anything?"

"Listen to your heart." He was all command now, brushing aside any equivocation. "You don't want to be alone in this. You want to be with me. I'm the man who'll look after you. I'm the man who'll always be there for you. The provider. The protector. But most of all, the one who loves you."

"Love…" she repeated, her voice wobbling over the tantalising word, her head reeling from the overwhelming force of arguments which were sweeping into all the empty places of her life and setting up unshakable occupation.

She forgot about backing away from him. He kept

coming—big, tall, powerfully built, sinfully handsome, intensely sexy, with a mind that saw obstacles as something to beat, nothing to stop him. And the truth was she loved him. She loved everything about him—this king amongst men.

He seized her upper arms. His eyes blazed with an indomitable will to win. "Stop all this destructive resistance, Nicole," he commanded in a voice that drummed through her heart. "Stop and remember what we felt when we came together. When we made our baby...yours and mine...together. It was right. Admit it!"

The intense blast of his passion poured a sizzling sense of rightness through every cell of her body. And wasn't he promising everything she had ever ached for?

Admit it!

She wanted to be Matt King's wife...wanted to become part of his extraordinary family...wanted their child to belong here.

His fingers pressed urgent persuasion. "Give us a chance, Nicole. Please...just give us a chance."

admiring her. . . tall, elegantly boned, darkly handsome, immensely sexy, with a mind that saw obstacles as something to beat, nothing to stop him. And the truth was, she found him. She . . . . him . . . thinking about meeting . . .

CHAPTER NINETEEN

DEAR Elizabeth,

I write this with great joy. Yesterday Nicole gave birth to a beautiful baby boy. He is to be called Stephen, after my father. Nicole insisted on it. She has a very strong sense of family tradition, which is very comforting to me. I know when I am gone, she will be the keeper of all I have tried to set in place. It is meaningful to her.

Every day I leaf through the family history she wrote for us and I can feel her love of it on every page, even to the way she placed the photographs. I hope she will add to it in the years to come, especially the photograph I am enclosing with this letter. Ah, the love and pride on Matteo's face, looking down at his wife and newborn son, and Nicole glowing the same feelings right back at him. It brings happy tears to my eyes.

This was a match truly made in heaven, though God knows they were difficult people to bring together. It was so fortunate they were blessed with a child to make them come to their senses and acknowledge what they were to each other. Well, you saw them at their wedding. Such strong passion between them. There will never be anyone else for those two.

I can rest content now. Alessandro, Antonio, Matteo…they have the right partners. And here I am with four great-grandchildren, two boys, two girls. Antonio and Hannah adore their darling daughter and no doubt she and Stephen will be splendid company for each other, born so closely together.

There is nothing like family. To me it is the keystone of our lives—our past, our present, our future. I know you feel this, too. I enjoy our correspondence very much, and I want to thank you once again for all your wise advice. Each night I lie in bed and I think of our family lines—yours in the Kimberly, mine here in the far north—and I see them thriving for a long, long time, Elizabeth. I go to sleep with a smile.

I am sure it is a smile we share.

With love,
Isabella Valeri King

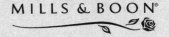

Three brand-new,
sinfully scandalous short stories

Regency
BRIDES

Anne Gracie, Gayle Wilson, Nicola Cornick

Available from 20th September 2002

*Available at most branches of WH Smith,
Tesco, Martins, Borders, Eason, Sainsbury's
and most good paperback bookshops.*

1002/29/MB46

URU 804
G3680

FREE!
2 Books
and a surprise gift!

We would like to take this opportunity to thank you for reading this Mills & Boon® book by offering you the chance to take TWO more specially selected titles from the Modern Romance™ series absolutely FREE! We're also making this offer to introduce you to the benefits of the Reader Service™—

- ★ FREE home delivery
- ★ FREE gifts and competitions
- ★ FREE monthly Newsletter
- ★ Books available before they're in the shops
- ★ Exclusive Reader Service discount

Accepting these FREE books and gift places you under no obligation to buy; you may cancel at any time, even after receiving your free shipment. Simply complete your details below and return the entire page to the address below. *You don't even need a stamp!*

YES! Please send me 2 free Modern Romance books and a surprise gift. I understand that unless you hear from me, I will receive 4 superb new titles every month for just £2.55 each, postage and packing free. I am under no obligation to purchase any books and may cancel my subscription at any time. The free books and gift will be mine to keep in any case.

P2ZEB

Ms/Mrs/Miss/Mr ....Initials...
BLOCK CAPITALS PLEASE

Surname ....

Address ....

....

....Postcode ....

Send this whole page to:
UK: The Reader Service, FREEPOST CN81, Croydon, CR9 3WZ
EIRE: The Reader Service, PO Box 4546, Kilcock, County Kildare (stamp required)